All rights reserved. No part of this book may be reproduced in any form or by any electronic or mechanical means, including information storage and retrieval systems, without written permission from the author, except in the case of a reviewer, who may quote brief passages embodied in critical articles or in a review. Trademarked names appear throughout this book. Rather than use a trademark symbol with every occurrence of a trademarked name, names are used in an editorial fashion, with no intention of infringement of the respective owner's trademark. The information in this book is distributed on an "as is" basis, without warranty. Although every precaution has been taken in the preparation of this work, neither the author nor the publisher shall have any liability to any person or entity with respect to any loss or damage caused or alleged to be caused directly or indirectly by the information contained in this book.

This is a work of fiction. Names, characters, places, and incidents either are the product of the author's imagination or are used fictitiously, and any resemblance to actual persons, living or dead, events, or locales is entirely coincidental.

Prologue

The events that I am about to recount took place in the year 2019. Many have speculated regarding these events: some are more accurate than others. But, there are some truths about that time that stand up to scrutiny. Following these events, professional wrestling would be banned from taking place in South Yorkshire for a term no less than ten years. Maybe it was for the best. For certain, I think there's something to be said about what happened of it being rather symbolic of the time it occurred. Everyone having their own agenda – seeking instant, individual success rather than working together as a team to build something. Everyone seeking to be that one person on top of the mountain and willing to kick every other person off it to get there. Anyway, I will let you come to your own conclusions about why what happened, happened.

Just for the record, all of the events which I am about to describe occurred, on a small independent professional wrestling event in South Yorkshire. All of the characters are real. As two famous film-making brothers might have said: out of respect to those who were involved, I have changed their names to crude pseudonyms. Out of respect for the family of the one guy who died and because I just couldn't write it any better than it actually unfolded, everything else has been described exactly as it occurred.

Chapter 1

The Incident

It is 4.17pm on the afternoon of Sunday, 13th October 2019. The West Duke Working Men's Club on Rotherham Road has never been quite so full. Well, at least not for a few months. And with the exception of big football matches, but that's a given. And that Phil Collins tribute. But, nonetheless, the room is over half full. There is a melting pot of people in attendance for the event.

First, are the young children, sat on the edge of their seats, watching with wide open mouths and wonder in their eyes. They know that they get more leeway with their parents, because it's a wrestling show and an unspoken suspension against the rule of shouting mean or crude things hangs in the air. Also, their parents are quite drunk. And, the kids take full advantage of this, berating the baddies for their weight or their ugliness, whilst trying to get high fives and hugs from their favourites. Sat beside them are their parents, laughing at their children's vulgarities and sitting back in their chairs, a bit tipsy and with a smirk on their faces which says, 'I'm not falling for this fake wrestling crap', which occasionally slips as they stare with blank faces at the action in the middle of the ring, as if a great truth has been revealed to them (it could just be the alcohol).

Sat behind them are a couple of dozen young men, all attired in dark wrestling t-shirts with wrestling slogans and logos inscribed on them. All look very similar: scraggly beard, messy hair, jeans and hoodie. They compete with each other to prove who reads the most wrestling websites and how knowledgeable they are regarding the latest goings-on in the wrestling world. They shout insider terms, such as 'botch', 'heel' and 'face' and chant things such as 'this is awesome' and 'fight forever' even at the slightest movement. These are the die-hard wrestling fans.

The room smells of the pungent combination of yeast, hops and barley. From every glass to every beer-soaked seat. On the front row, looking quite uncomfortable, is a man in his sixties, attired in a smart suit. Beside him, are two children and presumably the mother of the children. Every so often, he talks to the kids and asks them questions about what they're watching. Sometimes, they answer him, sometimes they don't and just continue to stare at the action, mesmerised. They seem comfortable with his presence, though, which suggests that he is some relation to them, perhaps their grandfather. He spends most of the show smiling awkwardly and trying his best to appreciate what he's seeing, seeming to be genuinely impressed at times. Although he seems out of place, he appears to be trying to make the most of his situation, perhaps by inviting his two young grandchildren and their mother along. This man is the mayor. He has been invited especially by the organiser to speak before the main event of the show.

In the centre of the room, the focus of everyone's attention, is a 16 foot by 16 foot wrestling ring, complete with its three ropes and a tattered canvass around eight feet below the ceiling, which restricts the wrestlers in what moves they can perform. Already, on two separate occasions, the feet of a wrestler have knocked a ceiling tile loose whilst the individual was being slammed or suplexed. Already that evening, has been a "no rules, falls count anywhere" brawl between the team of the Whacko Bros. – a team of football hooligan-inspired bald people – and the team of La Desesperada Atención and La lesión Constante. The latter team are young masked wrestlers and are greeted with much appreciation from the audience, even though Constante seems to be hobbling on his ankle and behaving somewhat erratically. It is rather charitable to say that this was a match. In the beginning , Atencion and Constante mount a little bit of offence, before Constante hurts his ankle, again, and then the Whacko Bros. proceed to throw them out of the ring and hit them with everything in sight, including beer glasses, beer bottles, chairs and tables, and even throwing them in to the women's toilets. The kids love this and the parents seem to not mind too much about the violence.

Later on in the show, the Whacko Bros. – along with a third wrestler – re-appear during someone else's match, and throw a group of three or four rough-looking individuals through the curtain and then scream at them to get back.

"Oh, look, Daddy," says one of the kids to their Dad. "Those two meanies are hurting some other people, now."

It appears that this was not a part of the show, as those participating in the wrestling match at the time simply glanced over at the scene, awkwardly, and continued with their match. The young men with black t-shirts on guffaw at the scene, completely forgetting about the match that is happening, and instead shouting things and staring at the people who have been unceremoniously thrown through the curtain. Shortly following them, are the wrestlers Matt Blast and the Whacko Bros. in shorts and t-shirts.

"Is this a work?" several of the black t-shirted young men wonder, referring to the occasions in wrestling when the 'booker' of a show will pretend to break down the fourth wall, only for that to be a part of the story, thus making those who believe they are better informed about professional wrestling confused.

The Whacko Bros. and Matt Blast occasionally shout at the men to "get lost" and "fuck off", showing flagrant disregard for the children in attendance. A couple of the men are recording the incident on their mobile phones. The wrestlers watch the men until they leave the venue, and then return behind the curtain from whence they came. Following the incident, there is a buzz in the audience which greatly overshadows what is happening in the ring. The competitors in the match, Mark Strong and Tommy Guinness, have spent much of this period of time putting on boring holds (what is known within the profession as a 'rest hold') to pause the action until the scene dies down. Once the men have left, they continue with their match. Following the match, the ring announcer apologises to the audience for the scene which has just taken place and the bad language used, explaining that there were some intruders in the changing room.

During the aforementioned incident, the Mayor has left his seat and apparently left the venue, along with his grandchildren and their mother. Nothing remarkable happens to match this incident until the main event. The main event has been changed from the previously advertised match between Huckle and Matt Blast to a six-man tag team match featuring Matt Blast and other competitors who have appeared during the event. Towards the end of the match, Matt Blast is making an impressive comeback for his team, knocking down two of his opponents and then the third, Michael Ali. A minute or so after being knocked down, Michael re-emerges from beneath the ring, where he has been hiding, wearing some sort of thick vest.

Immediately, the grins leave the faces of the parents in attendance. Their posture stiffens. As he stands up, the ring announcer, then the referee, stare at him with puzzled, blank expressions on their faces. The wrestlers in the ring perform a 'double down' in which both of them fall to the ground. Michael then grabs the microphone from the ring announcer and begins speaking.

"Don't anyone fucking move! This vest that I'm wearing is highly explosive and will kill everyone in here if you try to come near me or try to escape. I see the mayor in the audience, today…"

He points out a middle-aged man who is, in fact, not the mayor. Some in the audience have already left, whereas others are either standing or sitting on the edge of their seats. The wrestlers in the ring have seemingly not yet noticed that Michael is wearing a vest or whether it is fake and this is some sort of 'angle'.

"This event was a disgrace. How can the mayor of a major town be in attendance at this event, bring their children to this event? Women with their arms out and wearing skimpy clothes, wrestling? Men with their genitals almost on display. Obvious homo-erotica. This all ends now. None of this is according to the word of Allah. Allahu Akb...!"

Michael's hand has reached for a piece of string dangling down from the vest. Before he can finish his proclamation, he is tackled by one of the Whacko Bros. who connects with his shoulder into the side of Michael's head, which then hits the ceramic floor of the dance floor of the club. With Michael probably already unconscious, the Whacko Bros. then proceed to beat up Michael, throwing down dozens of fists and kicks to his head and body until there is blood leaking everywhere.

The children in the audience look on in shock, many of them crying. Some screaming. Their parents suddenly have moments of lucidity and try to protect their children from seeing what is happening. The rest of the audience, realising what has just happened and what is currently happening, rush for both the main door and the fire exits.

Chapter 2

An Im-Purr-Fect Crime

In this modest 9 feet by 9 feet room, the walls are painted a brilliant white, which has become less brilliant over the years in which grime, moisture and other dirt has built upon it. Here and there are markings and scuff marks where pieces of furniture must have struck it, either due to an excitable interviewee or a careless police officer re-arranging the furniture. In two of the corners, adjacent to each other, are pairs of filing cabinets, each with more files and paperwork stacked messily on top of each of them. There is a notice board in between them with various posters and leaflets pinned up, representative of different government initiatives. Also on the board, are instructions for evacuation in case of fire and even a poster demonstrating how to perform CPR. Below the notice board, is a green first aid box. The black carpet is thin and cheap, being lit up by the long plastic light on the ceiling which projects a sort of yellowish light in to the room. Finally, to the other side of the room, are two varnished, pine-topped tables put together to make one larger table.

On one side of these tables, is a man who appears to be in his thirties, who has a lot of stubble – at the point where it is difficult to decide whether it enters in to the domain of an unkempt beard – in addition to short shaven hair, a black t-shirt with a beer logo design on it and a thin grey jacket, which is open to show off his t-shirt. He slouches and looks down towards the table for much of the interview, dejected that his life has brought him to this situation. Sat beside him, is a genial man, apparently in his late-fifties or early-60s, in a smart but simple suit, with very gentle movements and a caring, careful demeanour. He still has a full head of hair, but his face is reddened due to some combination of long-term alcohol consumption and high blood pressure.

On the other side of table, are a man and a woman, both attired in police uniforms. They do not wear their police hats. The man appears to be in his late twenties whereas the woman appears to be in her early forties. They are in mid-conversation with the man across from them in the thin jacket and t-shirt ensemble.

"I can understand that this might be a very...embarrassing moment in time for you," the woman began, softly. "So, we do understand why you might not wish to speak about what happened. But, just to clarify, here is what we already have. We know that this man, Matthew Tarbuck, is a prolific drug dealer. We have been tracking him for some time, now..."

"Then, why haven't you arrested him?" interjects the man, rather aggressively.

"Well, Will, the reason we haven't arrested him is because we are aware that he is involved in a lot of drug operations with a lot of different people, and we want to find out who these people are. But our point is, that we know this is a powerful man and that he may have the ability to get people to do what they might otherwise not do."

There is a pause. As Will does not respond, the police officer's partner interjects. "We also know what you did...uh, we have surveillance footage from the Go Local Extra across the street. We know that you pleasured the cat. We just need to know why you did this. We already have a good idea why. But we just need to hear you say it. It will be of great benefit to you in your trial, or even before the trial if you can reach a settlement with the owner, if you could explain to us why you did this. The judge will look positively upon it."

Will sits still for a moment or two, before shuffling in his seat and looking up at his amiable solicitor. The solicitor nods to him. Will sighs and looks down, squarely at the table in front of him.

"T-Buck said I could have some free cocaine if I did that to the cat."

"And, just to be clear for the tape," the female police officer replied. "By 'T-Buck', you're referring to Matthew Tarbuck, correct?"

"Yeah."

"Thank you, Will," the woman said. "I know that can't have been easy for you. And, I do understand the impact that drug addiction can have on people. I have relatives who have struggled with it, so I...would like to imagine that I have some idea. But, by saying what you have today, it's going to hopefully help save lives. To save people like you."

"I don't think people like me are worth saving," mumbled Will.

"That's not true at all," the woman continued. "Once this is all done with, if you would like us to help you, we can. The judge may even recommend a course of treatment to help you. And then, when you're clean, you can do anything. You're still young. Only twenty-four. That's nothing. You could turn your life around and never look back."

Following the conclusion of the interview, the police officers shake hands with the solicitor and – demonstrating trust in the defendant – with the defendant himself. The defendant would go home until his trial was to be heard at the magistrates court, before perhaps testifying in the trial of the drug dealer at the Crown Court, a couple of months later.

The two police officers exit the room, and, after escorting the other two men to the foyer, walk down the hallway in silence. They walk through one set of doors, past a number of busy offices, and then through a second set of doors, all in complete silence, heads bowed, before entering into an office which bears, amongst other names,

SGT. JANE MULLIGAN and PC JAKE CARVER.

They close the door behind them, and then both let out audible sighs. Carver leans up against a filing cabinet.

"Well...that was..." he begins.

"Yeah," Mulligan responds, already knowing what he was thinking about. "Coffee?"

"Yes, please, ma'am."

Jane Mulligan, whilst she is the superior of Carver in the police hierarchy, willingly makes coffee for him, as she sees herself as much as a friend to her subordinates as a colleague or boss.

The policing world has been gripped in identity politics and draconian regulations designed to push a political agenda over the past few years. One of these forms of identity politics encourages female police officers to be resentful and jealous of their male colleagues. However, Jane has resisted this, as she recognises the importance of working together and forming bonds with her colleagues. She is also the beneficiary of some "positive discrimination", so there isn't exactly much for her to complain about, even if she wanted to. In truth, she feels rather guilty at being promoted above male colleagues due to her gender.

Jane knows exactly how to make the coffee for Jake, as she has done it many times. Two sugars and milk. Whilst she proceeds to make it, she wonders aloud, "I don't know why…how do people get into these sorts of situations? Even if you are a severe cocaine addict, how do you not stop yourself before doing something like that to a cat? I…just don't get it."

"Well," began Jake, receiving the cup of coffee from Jane, "I suppose…drugs can make people do some very strange things. Things that they wouldn't otherwise have done in a million years."

"Yeah," Jane continues. "That's definitely true. I just…he seemed like a decent guy, apart from that."

Jane walks over to the filing cabinets that Jake had been leaning on and pulls out a file, closes the file and continues, "One thing's for sure, in this job, Jake – you learn a lot about people that you wouldn't otherwise learn. The sides that you probably never wanted to know in the first place. But, that's our duty, I suppose."

A tall, grey-haired man with a slightly more detailed suit than Mulligan and Carver, very neatly dressed with a few extra pounds around his waistline, enters the office.

"I have another interesting case for you two," he began. "Murder at the West Duke Working Men's Club. As MIT are very busy with the Dalton Powerlines Case, I'm going to need to pass this on to you. Enjoy."

The man then passes a file to Sergeant Mulligan and leaves the office.

Chapter 3

Crimson Bulb

After having read through the case file and taken notes, Mulligan and Carver take the short drive to West Duke Working Men's Club. Even though the Club is only around half a mile from the police station, it is important to use the police car, for multiple purposes, including possible arrests and to easily access the police computer. As they enter the area, they see a crowd of a few dozen people crowded around the car park. Jane turns on the siren for a couple of seconds to clear the pathway. The people promptly make room for them to pass.

Mulligan and Carver exit the car, lock it and turn around to face the large group of people. It is clear from the expressions on their faces that many of them are deeply shook. There are even some young children, who are completely devoid of energy and have thousand-year stares on their faces. Next to the double doors are another couple of police cars and an ambulance. Considering that the victim is apparently dead, the pair wonder why the ambulance is necessary. A possible answer is found when Mulligan sees a paramedic from the ambulance speaking to and comforting some of the people huddled around the car park.

A Police Constable greets them and briefs them on what they have discovered so far. Whilst this is taking place, Jake looks around the room, and sees that the paramedics are in fact helping another man, who has apparently been injured in the incident. Then, looking over to the centre of the room, is a wrestling ring. As he has only ever seen professional wrestling on the television, it is surreal to him to see a wrestling ring in such a humble surrounding. Then, right in front of the ring, to his left, are two police officers, one of them kneeling over. In front of them, is what appears to be some sort of large animal carcass. But it soon turns out that it is the body of a man. Curiously, where the head is supposed to be, there only seems to be a dark crimson bulb. From this distance, Jake cannot very clearly make out what it is or what condition it is in.

As Jake and Jane get closer to the scene, a strong metallic smell enters their nostrils. They are very familiar with that smell: it is the smell of blood. Drying blood. Or 'the smell of death', as it is commonly known. The police officers inspecting the body acknowledge the presence of Jane and Jake. The body is attired in lycra shorts, knee pads and large boots. From the torso, it is clear that the man appears to be of Indian sub-continent heritage. Only from the torso and the legs is this clear, however, as what was once a head is now a mound of dark crimson liquid covering bone, with flaps of what can only be perceived to be skin drooping from it. Both Jake and Jane are startled as soon as they catch a glimpse of the skull, turning away for a few seconds. These are the trials of a police officer: the sacrifices they make. The combination of the gruesome image and the strong metallic odour of blood is something that no-one completely becomes accustomed to.

"Are the suspects in custody?" Jane enquires, calmly, once she has regained some composure.

"Yes, ma'am. They've been processed and should be in the holding cells, now."

Jane looks to her left and sees what appears to be a bulletproof vest. Wiring sticks out from it. It is covered in some sort of transparent wrapping.

"What's that?"

"That's a poor attempt at a bomb vest," the police officer begins, before rising to his feet. "So, what happened is, this…gentleman, Mr. Ali, was attempting to set off a bomb that he had made, in front of about a hundred people whilst this show was taking place. The bomb didn't work, as I say. Then, two wrestlers tackled him and beat him to death."

"Has the bomb squad been here?"

"Yes, ma'am. They came immediately. But it doesn't even resemble anything like a bomb, inside, so there is absolutely no danger. I'm not sure whether he was just trying to scare people or he was just really bad at making explosives."

"Have you taken statements from everyone?"

"Yes, ma'am. The staff, several of the customers, all of the wrestlers and everyone involved in the show."

"Suppliers?"

"The only supplier was the man who set up the ring. We took his statement, but as we have to leave the ring up for now, he's had to go home."

After inspecting the scene further and concluding the conversations with the other police officers, Mulligan told the officers to collect the evidence, bring the undertaker in and clear the scene. A few journalists from local media outlets turn up and Mulligan and Carver split up and give statements to each of them, staying close to the usual aura of officialdom and withholding judgement on many aspects of the case. Mulligan is very experienced at giving these sorts of statements, and confidently delivers them. Carver is also quite confident in doing so, but occasionally has to rack his memory for what he is supposed to say. As journalists often are, they are relentless and would keep asking questions for hours if they could, so Mulligan and Carver have to cut them off and get back into their police car.

After having driven around the corner and stopping at a traffic light, Mulligan asks Carver, "So, what do you make of that?"

Carver glances over to her and says, "Well, it looks like the victim was an amateur terrorist, probably radicalised on the internet, and was trying to make a statement. It didn't work out and he got pummelled to death, instead of blowing himself up. Thankfully."

"Thankfully?"

"Well, it's good that only he died, as opposed to how many would have died if he actually knew how to construct a suicide vest, properly."

"Well, yeah…good point. But I'm just wondering, if he was radicalised on the internet, how did he manage to construct such a shambles of a vest? Many of these websites and groups have pretty intricate descriptions of how to put one together. If he really was planning to use it, surely he would have made sure about it, first."

There is a pause, whilst Carver considers her point. "I don't know. He might not have been too smart. Or, as Steve said, he might have just been trying to scare people. We probably won't know until we speak to some people who know him. Like his parents."

Mulligan nods. "Then, there is the organiser of the event. He hired Michael. So, surely he should have known about it. He must be at least partially responsible. How do you just let someone into the changing room with a home-made bomb? In fact, how did anyone not see that?"

Chapter 4

An Unhappy Marriage

Jane Mulligan and Jake Carver are once again sat on one side of a table in the brightly-lit interview room with no windows. On the other side of a table, sits a solicitor, younger than the previous one, looking a bit worse-for-wear. Prior to this interview, his client has been talking a lot and making quite a scene, to the point where it was difficult to communicate with him and to decide what their strategy was going to be. The solicitor has come to the conclusion that this case is going to be a long one, which he probably won't enjoy very much, and will probably involve a lot of trying to convince his client to calm down and pulling him back from the brink. He hopes that he will be able to transfer the case on to someone else, or at least share duties with someone else in the LegalAid office.

Sat next to the solicitor, is said client. As he has been arrested in his home, and not being given much of an opportunity to change clothes, he wears very casual clothing. Clothing one might wear whilst sitting at home with a plate of nachos, watching cricket. Indeed – there appears to be some thick, sugary, red substance with the same consistency as salsa splashed on the front of his Sheffield Wednesday football shirt. A sports fan, indeed. But, seemingly, not a participant, as that same football shirt tightly wraps around a significant beer belly. The man has one of those beards where you can't tell whether it was grown intentionally or is simply the result of the owner being too lazy to shave. He has short hair. His age is difficult to ascertain – he could be aged anywhere between his late twenties and his mid-forties. Currently, he is engaged in his favourite activity: talking BS.

"I'm telling you, I know absolutely nothing about this. Mark Strong recommended him to me and he's done a couple of shows for me, he's always very quiet, there wasn't anything to suspect. He didn't talk to many people – he wasn't exactly a conversationalist – but he caused no problems and there was no reason to suspect that he was capable of anything like this."

"Who's Mark Strong?" Jake shot in whilst the defendant was taking a breath.

"Oh – he's just one of my regulars. But, I'll tell you who you should be looking in to…"

He jabs his finger at the two police officers' general direction.

"Tommy Guinness. Real name: Thomas Grayson. Another one of my regulars. He's had a problem with me for a long time. Last year, he kept showing up to my shows drunk, so I had to punish him by putting him in smaller roles, and also so he didn't hurt anyone or himself. Since then, he's had a real vendetta against me. He slept with my wife. And goodness…"

"Wait a minute," Jake interjects. "He's slept with your wife?"

"Damn right – he did, the little sh…" Sidney cuts himself off before he swears, as he wants to seem reasonable to the police officers. "Yeah."

"If he has slept with your wife and turned up to shows drunk, as you have said, why haven't you got rid of him? Surely, you have plenty of reason?"

"He's been threatening me. I'm afraid that he'll do something worse. If he was involved in what happened, here, then he has apparently already done something a LOT worse."

Jake and Jane exchange a tense glance.

"I must inform you, Mr. Sidney," begins Jane. "That it will look a lot better to a judge, if you tell us the complete truth, now. I am, of course, not prejudging what you have said, here. But, I think it is our duty to tell you this. If what you have said turns out to be false and we find out that you actually were involved, then this will probably force the judge to increase your sentence, and you may even be charged with obstruction of justice, in addition."

"I understand that, yeah," Sidney calmly replied, still attempting to emit an aura of trustworthiness.

"So, I am going to ask this question to you, one more time, Mr. Sidney. Did you have any knowledge of what Michael Ali was planning to do, yesterday?"

"I swear," Sidney begins in a solemn tone. "None at all."

Jake and Jane simultaneously sigh and sit back in their chairs with glum expressions on their face betraying that they feel that they are about to waste several hours interrogating someone who had nothing to do with the crime.

"Okay. That's all that we want from you at this time, Mr. Sidney. This interview concludes at 10.17am on Monday, 14th October 2019."

...

Carver and Mulligan disembark from their police car, and calmly walk down a few houses of a typical housing estate in the suburbs of Barnsley. As they walk past, they keep track of the numbers of the houses...82, 80, 78...Then, they arrive at 74. Even though council tenants are not particularly known for being fantastic gardeners – with the exception of the over-60s contingent – number 74 stands out as being particularly unkempt. The lawn clearly hasn't been tended to for several years, with parts of the grass reaching to 6 or 7 feet, as they crash into the front of the house. The grass is mixed in with an assortment of weeds, brambles, thorns, crawlers and dandelions. The entry way into the garden isn't much better kept. The gate is a small wooden variety, that was apparently painted some years ago, and has been chipped away at through wood rot and misuse. It tilts into the ground, which gives it a bit of a human persona, one which is tired of life and just wants to be put out of its misery. The front of the house's surface is covered in little grey pebbles as many council houses of that era are, or at least originally were.

Carver and Mulligan fight through the tundra, watching carefully where they place their feet, before arriving at the front door, with its miscoloured, half-open letterbox and glazed window. Carver and Mulligan both take a moment to adopt the persona of the friendly neighbourhood police officer, well aware of the shock and surprise that most people experience from having police officers at their front door, and then knock on the door three times, firmly but with restraint.

Knock, knock, knock.

Inside the house continues the trend of the outside of the house in being messy and unkempt. Right at the other side of the door, is a mountain of letters, take-away menus, leaflets and other junk mail. The carpet is stiff with the dirt that has been tread into it over many years. The outdated wallpaper is discoloured and stained. At the top of the stairs, past the handrail that is dislodged at the top, there are three rooms: a bathroom (the less that is said about that room the better), a bedroom and a third room, which is supposedly a bedroom, but appears to be simply a dumping ground for rubbish and long-forgotten possessions.

Inside the bedroom that is actually in use, lays a young man and a young woman. The man lies there for a few moments with his eyes half open, having been awoken by the sound of the police officer's knock. Not realising what it is, yet, however, he just stays there, wondering what has awoken him.

Outside of the front door, Mulligan glances back at Carver, before knocking again, a bit stronger this time.

Knock, knock, knock!

By this time, the young man realises what the origin of the sound is, but does not rush to his feet, being a bit annoyed that he has been awoken. Instead, he slowly moves the duvet off of him and sits on the side of the bed. Eventually, he gets to his feet, slowly and unsteadily, his bare frame trying hard to maintain stability.

At the outside of the house, Mulligan and Carver exchange another look, before Carver begins to peer into the front window, and Mulligan opens the letter box fully, shouting in, "Police! Please come to the door!"

This surprise shocks the young man into action, and he shouts down, "yeah!" Although, still quite groggy, the shout is croaky and not projected well. He then frantically looks around his room for some clothes to put on. He finds a pair of shorts and a t-shirt which he quickly puts on and then takes a moment to look for his sandals.

The young woman, who has been sleeping in the same bed as him, asks, "What's going on? What have you done?"

"Nothing," the young man replies. "I don't know what they want."

Outside the house, Mulligan communicates to Carver, "I'm not sure they're going to be coming to the door."

Mulligan knocks on the door one more time.

KNOCK! KNOCK! KNOCK!

She peers through the letterbox one more time, to see a young man sliding down the stairs, unceremoniously and in a way which suggests it was not planned and was actually rather painful. The man slowly gets up, holding his back, and walks over and unlocks the door.

As the door opens, Carver puts his mobile phone away and Mulligan sees that the young man is wearing only one sandal with the other at the bottom of the stairs. His eyes are half-open.

"Good morning, sir," Mulligan begins. "Am I speaking to Thomas Grayson?"

"Yes."

"Would it be possible for us to come in and speak to you for a few minutes about an incident which occurred, last night?"

"Sure," the young man says, and waves them in to follow him. He first re-attached the other sandel to his bare foot, before walking into the living room. Mulligan and Carver follow him in to see a room for which you can still recognise some sense of it being a well-decorated, pleasant room. Since then, it has been covered by a layer of dust, dirt, pizza boxes, old newspapers and dirty pots. The aroma is one of a mixture of the pungent smell of cannabis and sweat. Thomas picks up a small can of air freshener and sprays it liberally around the room, before making some space on the sofa for the two police officers to sit down. He next grabs a seat from the dining room table and sits down himself, across from the officers.

After getting settled, Mulligan begins to speak, again, "Thank you for inviting us into your home, Mr. Grayson…"

"No problem."

"…we just want to ask you a few questions about an incident which occurred last night, at the West Duke Working Men's Club. As you may already be aware, last night, a man by the name of Michael Ali was killed following what appeared to be his attempt at committing a terrorist attack. So, at this point…"

A petite young woman enters through the same door that police officers did, at this time, and walks past them into the kitchen. She is barefoot and wearing only a pair of knickers and a man's t-shirt, presumably Thomas', hanging loosely around her shoulders and extending almost to her knees.

"Good morning," she says, as she walks past the police officers and heads for the kitchen.

Carver and Mulligan stare at her and say hello, with Carver continuing to look at her, surprised, for a few moments longer.

"So…" Mulligan continues. "Uhh – are you a wrestler, too?"

Sandy calls in from the kitchen, "yeah."

"Were you at the same show that Tom was, last night?"

Sandy walks a bit closer and stares at Tom, for a while, trying to make sure that she doesn't say anything unhelpful. When satisfied, she replies, "yes."

"Okay. Well, you might want to take a seat, as well. It might be useful that we hear from both of you."

Both Mulligan and Carver have their notepad and pens ready to record information.

"First of all, what is your name, please, madam?"

"Alexandra Fox," she answers as she sits down on a chair next to Tom. "But, call me Sandy."

"Okay. I just want to get an idea of what you two were doing, last night…"

Both Tom and Sandy tense up for a bit.

"…at the wrestling event at West Duke Working Men's Club."

Tom and Sandy relax.

"If you could give me a timetable of events. Tom, if you go first, perhaps."

Tom inhales deeply and sits at the edge of the chair, rubbing his hands together.

"Sure…I…"

Tom is clearly trying to get a clear picture in his head of the events and to possibly overcome the after-effects of the previous night's alcohol consumption.

"…I got there at about noon, or just after. I talked to…other people on the show…"

"Who?"

"Uh...uhm...Matt Blast was one."

"He was another one of the wrestlers?" Mulligan asks, quickly noting down details of what he is saying.

"Yes. Also, Sandy..." he gestures to Sandy. "Joey der Verlierer, Donny Zaparcia...both wrestlers."

"What did you talk about?"

"Just...wrestling and life. The usual things. Nothing unusual. Then, I had a couple of drinks at the bar..."

"Before your match?"

"...yeah. I have quite a high tolerance."

"Well, I won't doubt that, but I sure hope you weren't driving, last night."

"No. Sandy drove me here. After that, I planned my match with Matt Blast, I waited backstage for a bit, we had our match, then Sandy drove me home."

"Did anything unusual happen, that night? Did anyone say anything or do anything that seemed out of place?"

Tom begins to shake his head, "No…" A moment of realisation. "The only thing I could mention is that Sidney had asked Matt to beat me up for real in our match."

"How do you know this?"

"Matt told me. He said that he wasn't going to do that. And he didn't."

"Well, that fits in to what we have been thinking," Carver interjects. "We've been speaking to Mr. Sidney in custody, and he says that you and him might have some sort of problem with each other."

"Yeah. He blames me for a lot of things. He doesn't seem to like me."

"Why does he keep booking you, then?" Carver enquires.

Tom shrugs. "I'm cheap and popular, I suppose."

"Well…" Mulligan continues. "Mr. Sidney says that you…slept with his wife."

With this, Tom becomes very uncomfortable and shuffles in his chair, looking around at Sandy. Sandy in return displays a look of shock and mild disgust at Tom. Tom shakes his head, as his eyes dart around in all directions.

"Look," Mulligan begins. "I don't really care whether you did or you didn't, but we're trying to find out why what happened last night, happened. We need to know whether you might have done this to get back at him."

"I – I didn't..." Tom stammers, but it is obvious that he is being obstructive, given the present company.

"Did you two sleep together, last night?" Carver asks, waving his finger between Tom and Sandy.

"Uhhh..." Sandy begins.

"It's just that...there's a very silly law that says, if a man sleeps with a woman and both are drunk, then the man is guilty of raping the woman."

"No. No, no, no," Tom blurts out. "Sandy just...was staying round because she was scared after what happened, last night. She wanted to be with a friend, y'know?"

Sandy nods. Mulligan seems concerned at Carver's approach.

"Okay," Carver continues. "The thing is...we have to report our suspicions. And, if that is what happened last night, I'm afraid that we're going to have to report it. However, you say that isn't what happened. So, if you were to show that you are a truthful person, then we would have no reason to doubt your word, would we?"

In reality, if Sandy did not wish to provide evidence, there would have been no case against Tom, but Carver knew that he had panicked him a bit. Tom rocks back in his chair, looks down at the ground and says,

"I did it. I did sleep with Sidney's wife."

"Okay. That's what he says, too…"

"But he said that it was okay. He and his wife are in an open relationship. So, I don't know why he would have a problem with it, now."

…

"But, to tell you the truth," Tom continues. "I cut it off with his wife a couple of months ago."

"Why?" Carver asks. "I mean, other than…did you feel guilty?"

Sandy looks at Tom expectantly, anticipating that he would say he felt guilty. Tom glances over at her before responding.

"No."

Sandy looks disappointed and increasingly irritated.

"I broke it off, because Sidney had been following us, myself and his wife. Before we spent an evening together, me and his wife would go to the supermarket. You couldn't imagine how many times we found him, hiding behind toilet roll, or in one of those little kids' sheds that you put in the garden, or behind the cereal. He got kicked out multiple times for knocking things over. Then, when we would ask him about it, later, he would always deny it."

"Do you think he was envious or did he just derive some pleasure from seeing you together?"

"I don't know! Maybe both. He's a very strange man. I couldn't possibly figure him out. But, that wasn't all. If we would go out for something to eat, he would either stand in the shadows outside the window or go to the same restaurant at the same time and pretend it was a coincidence. And then he would watch us. It was very uncomfortable. I even caught him creeping about in the back garden, here, a while back. I heard something knock on the window, and I thought it was a bird, so I went to close the window so it wouldn't come in. But, by the time I got to the window, there was nothing. I looked down and there he was, sprawled out on his back on the garden lawn. A bit like a dead bird, actually."

"Well, if he was doing all of this…" Carver began. "…why did you continue to go out with her?"

Sandy raised her eyebrows very high in anticipation.

"Well, I do like older women."

Sandy leapt up off the sofa with a big sigh and stormed off into the kitchen, unable to tolerate any more of the sordidness.

"They can be, uh...they know a lot more tricks..."

"I think that's all we need to know for now," Mulligan cuts him off, smiling warmly. Both Mulligan and Carver get to their feet, and Tom follows their lead.

"Thank you for your time, Tom. If we have anything more that we need to ask you, we may need to come back again, but hopefully that will be it."

Mulligan and Carver leave and begin walking down what remains of the footpath from the front door. Before they can reach the end of it, they already hear a loud female voice shouting from within the house. Following a short period of this, a male voice shouts back in return. The female voice then starts again and there can be thudding heard on the stairs. Mulligan and Carver can't quite make out, word-for-word, what the argument is about, but they guess and, after a couple of seconds of listening and then an exchange of glances, continue to their car.

Chapter 5

Sidney's Pinot Noir

Mulligan and Carver are back in the interview room with Sidney.

"We have spoken to Thomas Grayson," begins Mulligan, before taking a deep breath. "He has said that, you are in an open relationship with your wife, that he slept with your wife, and that you hold a grudge against him for that."

Sidney stares blankly at Mulligan for a second, then shakes his head. "Well, as you said, I am in an open relationship with my wife. We had planned for this sort of thing to happen. Why would I have a problem with it?"

Mulligan looks towards the table, and then laboriously raises her gaze again. "He says that, even though you pretend to be happy with the arrangement, you actually find it difficult as…she has been involved in more affairs than you have."

"Well, that isn't true. I'm doing fine."

Mulligan and Carver try not to spend much time considering that his appearance and personality may repel more people than it attracts.

"Well," Carver picks up. "Thomas also says that, you asked Matt Blast to attack him during their match on your show. Is that true?"

"No. I have no reason to do that. But, to be honest, I don't think Matt Blast likes Tom very much, so it may have just been an excuse…or, y'know, a veiled threat."

"I see," Carver nods. "Well, that's all for now. Thank you."

…

We are inside a council house not unlike the one owned by Thomas Grayson. This one is slightly cleaner than Thomas Grayson's and some care has been taken to keep it in good condition. However, on top of the clean surfaces and clean carpets, are piles of pizza boxes, cigarette packets and empty beer cans, mostly congregating around the sole armchair in the room.

Sidney is sat on the armchair, looking up at a woman in her late thirties to early forties. The woman is leant against the shelf above the fireplace with her left arm, whilst waving her right arm up and down in the general direction of Sidney.

"I can't do this, anymore, Sidney," she flung her head up into the air, dramatically.

"You can't do what?" Sidney asks her, a genuinely puzzled expression on his face.

She points with both hands towards the floor.

"This!"

Sidney is none the wiser, so just stares at her, wondering what "this" means, this time.

"You're lazy, you make a complete mess of the house all the time: I'm always cleaning up after you. You're always out with your mates…"

Sidney is reminded of the times he has claimed to be out with his "mates", which generally involves sitting in the corner of a pub, alone, drinking, mulling over the state of his life but pleased to have a couple of hours away from his wife and her abuse. He did once have friends; however, he stopped seeing them because whenever he would, his wife would throw a tantrum over the idea that he 'spends more time with them than you do with me', even though he was only visiting them for a few hours on a Sunday afternoon. Not wanting to put up with the abuse, anymore, he stopped going to see them, and they eventually lost respect for him due to him not having the courage to stand up for himself.

"…you don't take care of yourself. I think you're cheating on me. Are you cheating on me?"

"No."

"The reason I can't bring myself to have sex with you is because you're a slob…"

Sidney COULD detail all of the problems he has with his wife and that the reason he doesn't care about himself is because he feels powerless, helpless and depressed in his relationship. However, he has learned that she actually doesn't care about why he is behaving the way he is: she just expects to be able to speak to him however she wants, and for him to sit there and take it and apologise, for her to then not accept his apology and to carry on being abusive. He also knows that, if he does talk about his feelings, she will use it in an argument against him at some point in the future.

Another reason that Sidney does not stand up for himself is that, during the formation of their relationship, his then-girlfriend got him in to feminism. Realising how much she was interested in it and that getting into it himself could help them to get closer, he joined her in her passion. They would go to Lizzie Austin gatherings, together, where the male spouses would routinely be insulted and humiliated. But he was happy to be the butt of the joke, because, after all, "women had been oppressed for thousands of years", so it was only right for them to enjoy some empowerment. These feelings stayed with Sidney throughout their marriage, with Sidney putting her hours-long rants down to her being a "strong, empowered woman". Therefore, he was more than happy to subject himself to these rants and always felt that she must be in the right, somehow, and that he was always at fault. The result was that his chronic depression was completely ignored, whereas every little thing, positive or negative, that he said to her had to be carefully measured to ensure that it could in no way be considered in the slightest way, condescending or critical.

After over an hour of screaming and shouting at him, Sidney's wife takes a break in feigned despair (actually, she's just run out of things to say). Sidney takes this opportunity to try to solve the situation.

"Well, why don't you…"

Sidney's Wife's eyes widen in outrage that her husband is apparently talking back to her.

"...go out..."

Her eyes widen even more. *Is he telling me to get out of the house?*, she wonders.

"...and, er, have...be satisfied by someone else?"

Sidney's Wife's eyes widen even more. But, this time, there is a hint of excitement in her eyes.

"Are you suggesting that I have an affair?" she asks, shocked.

Now terrified of the rabbit hole that he has ventured down, Sidney meekly replies, "yes."

Sidney's Wife shifts her head back on her shoulders and is genuinely silenced and affected by something he has to say for once.

"I would consider the idea, Sidney, if only I didn't know that it was your way of trying to get rid of me. If you want to get rid of me, why don't you just say? Instead of dumping me on someone else?"

"I don't want to dump you on someone else," Sidney responds, laboriously. "I just think it would make you happier if you had someone else take care of that and then...we can just continue on as usual, otherwise."

Another lengthy pause, as Sidney's wife squeezes her lips together, manually, with her left arm that is resting on the mantlepiece and stares distantly into the mirror. A slight look of satisfaction creeps on to her face. Sidney sees it, and sees that she intends to take advantage of him, but has become so used to these daily humiliations by now that he just accepts it. His wife swings her head around to her husband with a new accusation.

"You're just suggesting this, so that you can have an affair, aren't you? You don't find me attractive, anymore, do you?"

Immediately ignoring the stunning hypocrisy of her words, Sidney replies, "No. I just think you would be happier, this way."

"How many affairs have you had since we've been married?"

"None."

"Really?"

This conversation continues on for some time, with Sidney's Wife trying to come up with several more ways to cast her husband in a dishonest or dishonourable light. However, in the end, she accepts the arrangement, as the opportunity is simply too good to turn down. Not only could she seek new sexual partners, but she could also cover up the affairs she had already had by claiming that they occurred after the arrangement was made. Then, over time, she could convince herself that that was the case and that she was entirely innocent. After all, if he's failing to meet her emotional needs, then she has to take care of them, somehow.

...

The doorbell on a very familiar door rings.

Ms. Sidney lets out a loud sigh, as she rises from her sofa where she has been watching *This Morning* on her television. For once, the house is clean and tidy: it appears that she has had a clean that very morning. She slowly rises from her chair, leaning forward, and using one hand to push up from her knee and the other to push up from the arm rest. She gets to her feet and staggers for a bit.

Knock, knock.

"I'm coming," she calls, somewhat irritated. She turns her head and sees through the frosted glass that there are two people who appear to be dressed in police attire. She straightens herself up, adopts a more regular gait and feigns a smile, and then walks swiftly towards the door. She unlocks the safety catch and then unlocks the door, opening it up and greeting the officers with a smile.

"Good morning," she greets with a broad smile.

"Good morning, Ms. Sidney," Mulligan responds, smiling back. "We're just wondering whether you would be happy to answer some questions about your husband."

"Yes, of course," she replies. "Please come in."

Ms. Sidney props the door open with her arm, and gestures with her other arm for the officers to enter the living room, still smiling broadly. Mulligan and Carver continue to smile as they enter, nodding somewhat awkwardly.

"Would you like to take a seat?" Ms. Sidney asks, gesturing towards the sofa.

The police officers assent and take a seat on the sofa, whilst Ms. Sidney sits on one of the dining chairs, opposite them. Mulligan and Carver get out their notebooks.

"Okay," Mulligan begins. "As we believe you're aware, your husband is currently in custody as we investigate a murder into a gentleman, that occurred at the West Duke Working Men's Club, last night."

"Yes."

"In order to determine possible co-conspirators, we are assessing the motives of the possible suspects."

"Okay."

"So...and I understand that this is very personal, but it is very important that we ask this...your husband says that you and he are in an open relationship. Is that true?"

Ms. Sidney raises her eyebrows, and, for the first time since the police officers arrived, expresses something other than warmth. Instead, she seems uncomfortable, rubbing her hands together, before placing them back in their original position on her lap.

"Yes. It is."

Mulligan nods gently, not wishing to upset her interviewee.

"Do you know, how your husband has felt about this? Has it raised any issues?"

Ms. Sidney purses her lips and looks over to the side.

"...no. In fact..."

She returns her gaze to the police officers.

"...He's actually been very affectionate, recently. Unusually so."

"Is he not usually affectionate?"

"Well, I wouldn't say he *isn't* affectionate. He's just been more so, recently. So, if he does have a problem with our arrangement, he's certainly done a good job of hiding it."

"Whose idea was it to have an open relationship?" Carver asks.

"His," Ms. Sidney nods.

Mulligan looks down at her notepad.

"Have you had…relations with a man named Thomas Grayson?"

Ms. Sidney blushes slightly and shuffles in her seat.

"Yeah. I – I have."

"Do you know of any tension between your husband and Mr. Grayson?"

"Well, my husband books him on his shows, so there can't be *that* much tension. But, I really don't know other than that. I don't think so."

"Is there nothing at all that you can think of? Any off-hand comment that he might have made about Thomas?" Carver enquires.

"Uhm…I've heard him complain that Tom has turned up drunk to a couple of his shows. But, if Tom has turned up to his shows, drunk, and he's still used him, then there can't be much tension. Because, I think most people would have had less patience with Tom under those circumstances."

...

It is a dark September evening. The inside of the Sidneys' house is pitch black, apart from the distant gleam of a streetlight. The house is entirely silent. But then, something abruptly breaks the silence. The sound of plastic dropping on to carpet with a thud, followed by the body of a man and then the words, "Oh, fuck! Who put that there!?" The voice belongs to Sidney. He scrambles to his feet and puts the fallen plastic object, a vacuum cleaner, back in a upright position. This is one of the few times that he has touched the vacuum cleaner. In fact, besides the time when he purchased the vacuum cleaner from ASDA, the only other times he has touched it have been when he has either walked in to it or moved it out of the way so as to not walk in to it. Oh, and there was the time when his wife got it out of the cupboard and insisted that her husband should use it whilst she was on a "girls' weekend away" but he simply put it back in the cupboard and didn't do anything of the sort.

Sidney opens the door of the small cupboard at the top of the stairs and sits there, cross-legged. There are narrow gaps in the door of the cupboard, but if one was to look inside, they would not see anything as it is too dark. And so, Sidney sat there and waited. Sidney checked the clock on his phone. The time was just after 1 'o' clock in the morning. From the tracker that he had put on his wife's phone, he believed that she would arrive within the next five minutes. Unfortunately for him, first they stopped at a petrol station, then they stopped at KFC (it was only for a short while, though, so it must have been the drive through – Ms. Sidney loves popcorn chicken), and then they even stopped at the side of a small road for fifteen minutes. Sidney imagined that Guinness' tyre must be flat. Having sat in this position for so long, his foot was starting to become numb, so Sidney awkwardly shuffled his legs around a bit within the small amount of space that the cupboard provided.

Finally, they approached the house. First, he could hear the tyres rolling over the road, nearby, and then the rumbling of the engine accompanied by headlights shining through the stained glass of the front door. Sidney puts his phone away and coughs so he won't have to do it later and risk drawing attention to himself. The engine shuts off and out get his wife and Guinness, conversing in muffled voices. Sidney feels a warm glow of embarrassment, anger and fear as he thinks that his neighbours are going to see the two of them being affectionate towards each other and showing excitement about spending the night together. His neighbours would know that he is a cuck.

Next, Sidney hears the key rattling in the keyhole, and makes sure he is especially quiet. Ms. Sidney and Guinness enter. There is ruffling of clothes.

"Wait until we get upstairs, Tom!" exclaims Ms. Sidney, playfully rebuking him.

They switch the light on, then go rummaging around the kitchen for some alcohol.

"I'm sorry about the state of the living room. I cleaned up just yesterday, but it's already a mess. Sidney doesn't take care of it at all."

"You should make him clean it."

"Oh – I try to. But, if I do that, it just gets worse and worse, until I have to give up and do it myself."

There is a rattling of glass.

"I'll tell you what – we'll drink Sidney's Pinot Noir. If he can't be bothered to clean up, then I'm going to drink his wine, instead."

"Ooh. Pinot Noir!"

After a few more moments, the lights downstairs are switched off again and the two make their way excitedly up the stairs. They enter Mr. and Mrs. Sidney's bedroom. By this point, Sidney has switched on the camera on his phone and is recording both the conversations and the action – well, the silhouettes of the two, really – on his phone. He records them closing the door but leaving it slightly ajar. He records them hastily pouring out the wine and taking a sip. He records them continuing their conversations about him, talking about how bad his hygiene and laziness is. He records the silence interrupted only by the sound of fabric rustling when they undress. And then, he records the sounds of them having sex.

As he hears them gradually getting more and more into their encounter, a series of feelings bubble up in him. Sadness slowly turning to depression. Fear slowly turning to panic. Anger slowly turning to rage. Awkwardness slowly turning to sexual arousal. When he's sure that they're too focused on each other to notice anything else and are making enough noise, he decides to leave the relative safety of the cupboard, silently opening one of the doors. He then tiptoes along the landing, making sure to only stand on the either the edges or where he thinks the beams are, so as to minimise any creaking of floorboards. On one occasion, he does make a floorboard audibly creak, but there is enough timber creaking in his bedroom for the two to not notice it.

Over the course of the next few minutes, he gradually builds up confidence to get closer and closer to the door until he reaches the ajar door.

By this time, Ms. Sidney has mounted Guinness, is moving up and down on him and is screaming, increasingly loudly. Adrenaline courses through the body of Sidney as the fabric around his groin tightens. He continues to look on and record.

Suddenly, Guinness pushes himself up with his hands and stares directly in Sidney's direction. Ms. Sidney follows Guinness' daze. Sidney backs off in shock.

"There's someone there!" shouts Guinness.

His heart now racing, Sidney clenches the phone in his hand and turns around, hitting his knees on the vacuum cleaner, again. He shuffles round on the spot for a while, before deciding that the window in the box room will be his means of escape. His phone pinging and being pursued by a naked Tommy Guinness, who himself trips over the vacuum cleaner, Sidney runs in to the bedroom and opens the window, which opens vertically as opposed to horizontally like most windows in the house. Still, the gap is still very small for the top-heavy Sidney to fit through. With Tommy now at the door of the bedroom and with access to the light switch, Sidney dives head first through the window. Guinness darts across the room as Sidney manually pushes his flaps of fat past the window frame. Just as he is about to break free and get through the window, Guinness grabs the bottom of his left foot.

In a panic, Sidney waves his feet around like a pig that knows it's been chosen for the slaughter. Getting free for the moment, Sidney takes advantage and flops out of the window on to the sloped shelter at the front of the house. He rolls down and grabs the drainage pipe to break his fall, part of which falls with him. A garden full of thorny bushes and overgrown weeds breaks his fall. With not enough time to untangle himself, Sidney simply removes his t-shirt and runs through the thorns, snagging the bottom of his tracksuit bottoms on the thorns. Sidney hears the sound of a bang on each of the steps, becoming progressively louder and closer. He quickly slips down his tracksuit bottoms, pulls them over his trainers and runs off down the street.

Feeling the brisk, chilly air on his bare torso and thighs, Sidney races down the street as fast as his unfit legs can carry him. Knowing that Tommy is much younger and fitter, he knows that he must find somewhere to hide. Luckily, it is the middle of the night, so that should be easier than it would otherwise have been. He looks across the street to see his favourite local supermarket outlet. *Shop = big bin,* he thinks, racing across the empty road. His heart jumps with joy as he sees that he was actually right, and there is in fact a big bin behind the shop. He opens it up and, after a couple of attempts, manages to roll into it. This is where he stays for the next half an hour to ensure that Tommy truly has lost him and is not continuing to look for him, and to figure out how he is going to get to his car without being seen in his underwear by...well, anyone.

Chapter 6

Alone Time

Mulligan and Carver's next stop is to the parents of the victim / terrorist, Michael Ali. Having already been informed of their son's death, his parents are waiting for Mulligan and Carver to arrive to explain the details and, if possible, to answer a few questions. His parents live in a high-rise flat in Doncaster. As Mulligan and Carver approach the block of flats, they are confronted by a "gang" of kids, spitting in their general vicinity and bragging about the crimes that their parents, older siblings and grandparents have been imprisoned for. Mulligan and Carver firmly tell them to disperse. Surprised by such firmness, they do indeed back away. Once inside the foyer, for the lack of a more descriptive term, of the block of flats, the police officers come across another group, this time of young men. The men are extraordinarily quiet, as if the officers have just interrupted a conversation that they did not want to be heard having.

"How are you gentlemen, today?" Mulligan asks, politely. They all murmur that they are alright.

"What are you talking about?" Mulligan enquires, with a heightened tone of curiosity.

"Nothing much," one replies. "Just planning our night."

"And, what do you have in mind?"

"We're going to go to the club in town."

"Ah. The Wet Fish?"

"No. The other one. The Noise Room."

"Cool. Well, have a good night."

They all say thank you.

Mulligan turns back around to the lift for a couple of seconds, presses the button, and then turns back around to the young men.

"Say…If me and my partner here were to search you, we wouldn't find any…drugs? Weapons..? On you?"

"Naw, naw," they say in unison.

Then, one blurts out, "Yo. That's racist, man."

"Drugs are racist?" Mulligan asks, confused.

"Naw. Searching us 'cos we're black, innit?"

"Possession of restricted substances is an offence for white people, as well, you know."

"I mean, SEARCHIN' black people, specifically."

"Well, I didn't say I was going to search you. But, if I was going to search you, the fact that you're congregated around the entrance of a block of flats and are suspiciously quiet, as if you were not even engaging in any conversation, would be much more motivation to search you than what colour you are. But, no – today, as you may be relieved to know, I am not going to search you."

Mulligan walks into the lift. Carver then turns to them, "Just make sure you don't sell any to those kids out there. We don't want to be back later tonight to arrest you for supplying drugs to one of them and killing them, do we?"

The group don't say anything. Carver then joins Mulligan inside the lift. When both Carver and Mulligan are both safely inside the lift and moving in an upward direction, Mulligan disconnects her radio from her belt, presses the button and says, "Anyone in the area of Balby. There are some young men and teens at the bottom of the staircase, who are likely possessing drugs. Have a word with them and keep an eye on them, please."

The lift opens a few floors below where the officers are heading. An elderly woman walks in and addresses them, "Are you going up or down?"

"Up," the officers reply in harmony with a warm smile.

"Oh. Well, I'll get in, anyway. There's no sense waiting out there."

"Which floor do you want?" Carver asks.

"Ground, please."

Carver presses the button on the side of the lift labelled 'G'.

"Did you see any of those kids down there when you came up?" the woman asks.

"Yes. We saw some young men," Carver responds. "But you don't need to worry about it. I don't think they'll cause you any trouble and we have officers keeping an eye on them."

"Yeah. They're always doing drugs and making a racket at night," the woman continues. "I don't know who their parents are. I would never have let my kids behave that way."

The woman then looks up at them sharply, and her eyes widen, "Are you here about Michael?"

"Michael Ali. Yes, ma'am," Mulligan replies.

"I heard what happened," the woman shakes her head, gently. "I've known his parents for a long time. Nice people. They make me dinners, sometimes. Sometimes, the worst things happen to the nicest people. It really is a shame."

The woman clearly seems touched by the subject, and may have been shedding a tear, but as she had her back to the officers, it was difficult to tell for sure, even with the blurry image cast back from the metal door of the lift.

Soon after, the lift arrives at the floor of Michael's parents and the officers make their way out.

"Look after yourself, madam," Carver offers.

"I will, dear. Don't worry. And give my best to the Alis. I'm Jennie Fulton."

"We will," Mulligan smiles at the woman.

Mulligan and Carver walk down the corridor and knock on the door labelled 2704. Shuffling can be heard followed by a muffled, female voice. The sounds of steps on carpet can be heard coming progressively closer. Next, a quiet, sliding sound of metal can be heard. Mulligan and Carver look and smile at the small, black, glass peephole on the front of the door. Some rattling of a chain follows, and then finally, the door opens to show a short, chubby, middle-aged woman of Indian sub-continent origin, who has tears in her eyes but is not currently crying.

"Hello," she forces a smile.

"Mrs. Ali?"

"Yes."

"I'm Sergeant Jane Mulligan and this is Constable Jake Carver from South Yorkshire Police," Mulligan says with a light smile, as both officers respectfully remove their helmets. Jane's voice then lowers, "We're here to discuss your son."

"Yes. Of course. Please come in."

Mulligan and Carver follow the woman into the living room, where a middle-aged man, also rather chubby and of Indian sub-continent heritage, is sat. Both have very grim, beaten expressions on their faces. Furthermore, it appears that Mrs. Ali has started crying, again. She reaches for a tissue from a cardboard box of tissues and sits next to the man – presumably, her husband, Mr. Ali – who wraps his arms around her shoulders to comfort her.

"Mr. Ali?" Mulligan asks. The man nods. "Do you mind if we sit down, here?"

"No," the man mutters and gestures towards the second sofa. The sofas are positioned adjacent to each other with the door to the living room in the corner that they both share.

"First of all, we would just like to offer our condolences on behalf of ourselves and South Yorkshire Police," Mulligan nods. Mr. Ali meekly smiles and Mrs. Ali whispers, "thank you."

"We won't take up much of your time. We just want to ask a few questions regarding Michael."

As neither of the parents object, Mulligan continues in a soft tone. Both her and Carver have withdrawn a notepad and pen.

"As I believe one of my colleagues has…said: last night, Michael appeared to be about to detonate a home-made explosive vest in what appears to be a terrorist act. So, we just want to ask a few questions about that. Firstly, were you aware that Michael was involved in any extremist activities? Or, did he express any extremist views to you, such as hatred of white people, women – anything at all?"

"Michael was always very respectful of everyone," the father began. "I have never known him to hate anyone like that – no."

"There was that one time," the mother raises her head. "At school…"

"Well, yeah…" the father begins to interrupt, dismissively.

"…He lost his temper with his teacher, once. But that wasn't really his fault."

"His teacher was constantly saying racist things – defending the British Empire – all sorts."

Mulligan takes a deep breath to ask more about the incident, but the father continues.

"Michael is a very devout Muslim and he's proud of his Bangladeshi heritage."

"What exactly did Michael say or do when he lost his temper, do you know?"

The father pauses for a moment, takes a deep breath, and says, "He DID say a few things that he later regretted and apologised for. He said that white people are mass murderers and should be ashamed of themselves. That sort of thing. I told him that he needed to apologise and he did. But I think it's understandable for him to feel angry when his teacher kept going on like that."

"Absolutely," Mulligan says. Whilst she does not really agree, Mulligan feels it is important to stay on the parents' side if she is going to encourage them to open up to her. "Was that the end of the situation? What happened then?"

"The school put Michael in a different class. They never did anything about that teacher, though."

Mulligan and Carver sit with the parents for around ten or fifteen more minutes, asking about many things, including his group of friends, his mosque, whether he enjoyed putting things together with his hands, books that he reads, his hobbies and whether he spent a lot of time using the internet.

"Michael did spend a lot of time on his computer," the mother began. "He's a student in Media and Performing Arts, so a lot of his work is putting together little films on his computer. I have to remind him to take a break, sometimes, from it. He's very hard-working."

…

A few months ago, Michael and his parents are stood up in their living room. His parents are dressed up in their coats and scarves with both carrying an umbrella, his mum carrying her handbag and his Dad rattling his keys in his hands. Michael is wearing casual clothes and no coat, and is wearing Spongebob SquarePants slippers.

"Okay, Michael," his father begins, sternly. "By the time we get back, I want those dishes to be clean, dry and put away."

"Yes. No problem."

Michael's parents then slowly make their way through the front door, lock the door and get into their car. The engine rumbles and they drive down the drive, before the tarmac can be heard underneath the car's wheels, gradually quietening as the car gets further away.

By this time, Michael has already abandoned his father's request and has locked himself in his bedroom with his laptop. He told his parents earlier in the day that he had planned to complete his university project, but his father insisted that he clean the dishes, pots and pans, anyway, whilst they were out. But this project is too important to Michael. He simply cannot be wasting time on menial tasks such as that when there is important work to be done. It is important that Michael impresses his teachers with his project. And, to do that, he must expend as much time as possible on it.

Set up on one side of Michael's bedroom is a tripod with his mobile phone affixed to it. He has planned to buy a professional camera at one point. However, his teachers have assured him that the mobile phone is good enough, as it reflects the gritty nature of the story that he wants to tell. Facing the tripod from the opposite side of the room is a makeshift green screen. In fact, it is simply a bed sheet that has been hung from a wooden structure that he constructed in the back garden. Again, Michael feels that this needs to be improved. But, again, his teachers are pleased with the "down and dirty" look of it, and did in fact provide advice on how to construct it. Therefore, Michael feels confident that they will be satisfied with it.

For this production, Michael has also gone to the extent of buying a costume for himself. This takes the form of a traditional middle-Eastern robe and a head scarf. He wears this to demonstrate his Islamic heritage, as this will be a film which draws from his people's cultural background. Having everything he needs set up, Michael walks over to his tripod and clicks on his phone, before tapping on the motion capture function and then returning to the front of the bed sheet, under the yellowish light coming from his bedroom light, and sitting cross-legged facing the camera. Michael straightens his back out and places his hands on his knees. Finally, he adopts a much more serious and sombre facial expression, takes a deep breath and begins to speak.

…

"Salma has a really beautiful door curtain. Did you see that?" Ms. Ali asks her husband.

"I did," Mr. Ali replies, steering the car into the drive. "It was very nice."

It pains Mr. Ali to admit this. He usually doesn't enjoy going around to his brother's house: his brother is a successful barrister making more than double his salary and, as a result, has a much bigger and much more well-decorated home. But his brother invited them around, probably on the insistence of his brother's wife, Salma, and Ms. Ali had insisted, being close friends with Salma. It has all left a bad taste in Mr. Ali's mouth.

"I hope Michael has sorted out the washing up," he sighs. "I can't be bothered with it, tonight, to be honest."

As Michael's parents are parking in the drive, Michael himself is still upstairs on his laptop, headphones on, having been watching back and editing his video.

"…the governments of the United Kingdom are mass murderers. They have slaughtered our people. All for oil. They enter the caliphate of Mohammed to steal our precious resource and do not care about the wellbeing of our people…"

By this time, Michael's parents have entered their living room and his mother has begun to hang up her coat. Mr. Ali heads straight for the kitchen to have a look at Michael's handiwork. As he suspected, the same thing that happened last week, has happened this week. The dishes are clean. Mostly. Admittedly, the job does appear to be rushed and there are some which still have areas that are not as clean as they should be, but they are just about clean. However, once again, it appears that Michael has quickly done them, gone back to doing whatever else he was doing, forgot to dry them and forgot to put them away. Also, he has not dried around the kitchen, so there are suds dripping down the counters. Mr. Ali lets out a big sigh. As he is taking it all in, Ms. Ali walks up behind him and looks at the work that Michael has done for herself. She lets out a sniff of laughter.

"Same, again," she says.

"Yeah," Mr. Ali responds in a downbeat tone. "Same again."

Mr. Ali then heads to the bottom of the stairs.

"Don't be too harsh on him," his mother says. "He IS doing his uni work."

"I'm not going to be," his father mutters. In truth, her request makes him more irritable, not less.

"Michael!" he calls up.

No response.

"MICHAEL!"

Still no response.

Mr. Ali then walks up the stairs, not something he wanted to do before he had had the chance to have a rest on the sofa for a few minutes, and approaches his son's door. He knocks.

"Michael!"

Still no answer. Mr. Ali opens the door to find his son, laying on his bed with his laptop open. As soon as they lock eyes, his son's eyes become much wider and he hastily closes his laptop and puts it to the side, before throwing off his headphones. Mr. Ali, knowing what is going on, simply raises his hand, turns away and closes the door.

Once Mr. Ali has made it back downstairs, he hangs his coat up and walks over to the kitchen, where his wife is busy drying the cupboards and the dishes, pots and pans. He opens the fridge and takes out a carton of orange juice. Having then checked in the cupboard for a glass, he realises that there aren't any in there so looks over to the sink area. Ms. Ali has noticed what he is doing and hands him a glass she has finished drying. Mr. Ali then proceeds to pour some orange juice in to the glass and takes a sip.

"What did he say?" asks Mrs. Ali.

"Uhh…I'll talk to him later. He's having a little…private time," her husband replies with a wink.

…

"I just can't imagine Michael being capable of anything like that…" Mrs. Ali says, her eyes darting across the floor.

"Someone must have coerced him in to doing it," Mr. Ali speculates.

"Well, that's what we're trying to find out," Carver responds. "That's why we need to know exactly who he has been around, recently. Is there anyone that you have noticed him spending more time with, recently?"

"He's just been going to uni, doing his uni work at home, here, and doing his wrestling, and that's it…" the father continues.

"That wrestling promoter…" the woman says, quietly. "The scruffy guy."

"Maybe," the father continues, looking blankly into the distance.

"Do you know the name of this man?"

"Yes," the father replies. "Mr. Sidney. Mr. Sidney was his name. He took Michael out to Frankie & Benny's this past weekend. I don't like the look of him. He doesn't seem to be the best person for Michael to be hanging out with. Very…"

"…sleazy," his wife continues. "I would talk to him, if I were you."

"We are already speaking to this man, as the incident did occur at his event. So, we will speak to him about this. Frankie & Benny's, you say?"

"Yes. At that big retail park."

"We tried to discourage Michael from being around him as much. But, I suppose he's – or was – kind of Michael's boss. So, I didn't know what to do."

The police officers go over a few more details with the parents, then Mr. Ali collects Michael's laptop from his room. He takes longer than would be expected for such a simple task, which makes the police officers believe that he might not be exactly sure where Michael had put his laptop. Mr. Ali does eventually re-emerge with the laptop, his eyes clearly wet, and hands the laptop to the police officers. Mulligan and Carver say their goodbyes, mention Jennie Fulton's well wishes and leave.

Chapter 7

A Happy Baked Potato

"Michael was always saying things like that!" Sidney exclaimed.

"This was backstage at shows?" Carver asked.

"Backstage; before the shows when we're setting up; after shows; whenever we would go somewhere, like to a restaurant or something…"

"So, you DID go to a restaurant with Michael?" Sullivan interjects.

"Yeah. I go to meals with a lot of the people I work with. Meals, we go out for a drink; we go paintballing; escape rooms. All sorts."

"Okay. And Michael made these sorts of comments when he was with you in these places?"

"Yeah."

"The problem is, Sidney," Mulligan continues. "…the fact that he said these so many times in your presence and you never reported them. I understand that it can be difficult to talk about people who are your friends…"

"Well, I wouldn't…"

"...or your employees, whatever it is. However, one of the ways in which we catch individuals such as Michael and prevent things from happening, such as what happened last night, is by reporting from the public."

"I understand that," Sidney says, softly, giving off the aura of repentance, amongst other things.

"And, given that you knew all of these things that he has said and didn't do anything about it, in addition to the incident occurring on your show when the Mayor was in attendance, may cast doubt on the idea that you weren't involved in this, as you say you weren't."

"I wasn't!" Sidney exclaims in indignation. "Look – I know that I have made a mistake in not reporting it. It's as you say – it's difficult – I didn't know whether to take it seriously or not. I thought he was just a troubled kid. No-one ever thinks this sort of thing is going to happen with someone they know. Everyone else that was on the shows – all the wrestlers and everything – heard him say all the exact same things and they thought the same. No-one ever thought he was being serious."

...

"Turn left…Follow the road for 150 yards…Then, you have reached your destination."

Mulligan and Carver park their car in front of a small strip of shops. Lined up next to each other are a corner shop, a fireworks shop that appears to be closed and a pharmacy. Just to the right of the corner shop is a black wooden door. The concrete in front of all of this is cracked with weeds growing from the cracks. The area around them is residential, with a row of small terraced houses opposite.

The officers walk through the black wooden door and walk up some dirty, uncarpeted steps before walking through another wooden door. As they get closer, they can hear voices echoing off the walls of the room they are approaching, as well as a springing noise which resembles the sound of a mattress. Then, a crashing sound. Then, someone shouting, "One! Two!..Two!"

Mulligan and Carver enter the room and have a brief look around. The room is not decorated, save for a layer of white paint which is unevenly spread across the walls. Metal beams cross from one wall to the other. The floor is just barely covered with thin, dirty carpet tiles that don't look like they have been vacuumed or cleaned since they were put down. Some of the walls are covered with posters featuring young men and the word 'WRESTLING' in large letters at the top of each one. Some of them have a very old-school design – monochrome, orange and black, with bold text announcing the matches for that night. It is notable that the dates on those posters go back much further than the other ones, some as much as 40 or 50 years. The air is thick with the smell of sweat that had long been soaked into every surface – the carpet, the walls, the plastic seats and, of course, the ring. Indeed – at the opposite end of the room, was a three-rope wrestling ring. It looks similar to a boxing ring, with the exception of one less rope and pads in different places. To Jake, this is a fascinating place, transporting him back to being a 10-year-old boy when he would watch wrestling on the TV on Saturday and Sunday mornings. To Jane, it is an interesting curiosity, but not enough to distract from her purpose.

All of this visual information has transmitted within a couple of short seconds, before they are both greeted by a chubby bald man who resembled a baked potato. He is a happy baked potato, though, grinning from ear to ear as he greets the two police officers.

"Good afternoon," he greets.

"Good afternoon," Jane says. "Are you Mr. De Verlierer?"

"I am, yes."

The two officers shake hands with the man.

"So, would it be possible for us to speak for a short while about the incident that occurred, two nights ago?"

"Of course," Mr. De Verlierer said. "Shall we go into this room, here?"

Joey De Verlierer, to give him his full name, gestures towards a room that is adjacent to the entrance to the room they are currently in. Mulligan and Carver follow his cue. Mulligan and Carver ponder how peculiar it is that Joey is so jovial, so shortly after the death of one of his acquaintances, in such a brutal way. Then again, they countenance, Joey had given off the aura of a man who has a lot of time on his hands: a man for whom meeting two police officers could be very exciting. Still, Joey seems nervous – his movements are jittery, his speech unnatural.

The three go through to the next room, through the door frame with no door and continue their conversation.

"This should only take a few minutes, sir," says Mulligan.

"No problem," Joey smiles.

"I take it that you are aware of what occurred on Sunday night, at Sidney's show, regarding Michael Ali?"

"Yes...I was there."

"We understand that Michael had been making a series of...extremist comments. Is this something that you're aware of?"

"Oh, yes." Joey's face lightens up as he revels in the ability to feel useful. "He was always saying things such as the British and American governments being murderers and how...uh, Muslims will out-populate white people and wipe them out."

"Anything else?"

"Various things to do with Islam taking over the world..."

"Okay," Mulligan nods as she notes down what Joey has said. "We ask members of the public, whenever they hear or see something which may possibly be associated with extremist ideology to report this to the police by either contacting your local police department or on our non-emergency hotline by dialling 111."

Joey's face drops as he begins to realise that this meeting may not be as fulfilling as he had hoped.

"We're not going to take any further action, now, but we just want you to keep this in mind for future reference."

"Oh, well…" Joey splutters. "…I wasn't sure what…what to make of what Michael said…"

"I understand," Mulligan continues. "But, in future, if you do hear anything like that being said, regardless of whether they're being serious or not – it might just be nothing, but there's always a chance of it not being – then just let us know and let us figure it out. Okay?"

"Yeah."

A bit crestfallen, Joey nods. "Would you like to speak to any of the others who were at the show, last night?"

"Yes, please."

The three begin to walk into the larger room. In the ring, are a couple of young men as well as a couple of men who appear to be about ten years older. The two young men are performing a sequence but seem to be a bit clumsy as they are clearly inexperienced. Meanwhile, one of the older men, who has short hair, is wearing a vest and has a well-put-together upper body concentrates on what they're doing but does not speak. To his left, is another man, around the same age, but clearly much more chubby with long hair which doesn't look like it's been tended to for twenty years and attired in black and white gear with the logo of a popular martial arts and fitness brand plastered across both his shorts and his t-shirt. Unlike the other man, he has a lot to say, and is constantly barking orders at the two young men.

"Would you like me to call them over?"

"Just give them a little while to finish what they're doing. It's okay," Mulligan responded.

Back in the ring, the two young men have completed what they were attempting and the fat man with long hair is giving them more advice. The other man interjects at various points to say what he wants to say.

"The two who were there, last night, are Matt Blast and Danny Zaparcia," Joey confirms, gesturing towards the two older men.

Matt and Danny then do the sequence that the other two were attempting, just a moment ago. However, at several moments throughout, Danny stops, having forgotten what he was supposed to do, and is promptly reminded by Matt. Zaparcia gets increasingly annoyed. Finally, having watched enough of the masterclass, and Matt Blast having exited the ring and speaking to one of the young trainees, Mulligan and Carver approach.

"Don't worry about Danny," Matt begins to the trainee. "He has a huge ego. Just focus on what we talked about."

Matt Blast looks around to see Mulligan and Carver standing there. His eyebrows raise.

"Mr. Blast?" Mulligan enquires.

"Yes."

"Would you mind if we had a brief talk about what happened last night with Michael Ali?"

"Of course not."

Matt Blast then follows the police officers over to the area that they had had the conversation with Joey, a moment ago. The conversation goes similarly to the one with Joey, with Matt admitting that he had heard Michael making extremist comments and the police officers warning him that he should report anything like that to the police, in future. However, he does make one comment in relation to how Sidney had asked Mark Strong to beat up Tommy Guinness, but himself and a couple of others had to step in to prevent it from happening. A similar conversation occurred a few moments later with Danny Zaparcia.

Whilst the conversations have been ongoing, Mark Strong has entered the training centre. Mark Strong is a short man, around 5 foot 7 in stature, with a bald head and a permanent look of annoyance on his face and a miner's cap on top of his head. The officers decide to question him before he becomes busy.

"Hello. Mark Strong, is it?" Carver introduces himself.

"Yes. How can I help you?"

Even though he is short, Strong moves like a man much taller in stature with movements demonstrating swiftness, assertiveness and a bit of aggression.

"We would just like to ask you about what happened, last night, regarding Michael Ali."

After having the identical conversation regarding Michael's extremist comments, with Mark being a bit more stern in his response to his telling off for not reporting it to the police, they come on to the subject of Sidney asking him to beat up Tommy Guinness in their match for his relationship with Sandy Fox.

"Yeah. Sidney did say that. I didn't do it, though. I'm not like that."

"So, what did happen?"

"What do you mean?"

"Was Sidney annoyed with you for not doing what he had asked?"

"No. I don't think he knew the difference, anyway. I work a bit stiff, anyway – a bit…I hit quite hard, in general, so I don't think Sidney knew the difference. I just sat down before the match with Tommy and explained what Sidney had asked me to do and told him that I wasn't interested in doing it. Then, we went out and had our match. Who was it that told you about this?"

"One of your colleagues."

"Was it Matt Blast?"

"Yeah," Carver let slip.

"Yeah. He came up to me after knowing about it and asked me not to do it. I'm sure he would have said that he told me not to do it, but that isn't possible. But, I wasn't going to do it, anyway."

"Okay. Understood. Thank you for your time, Mark."

The police officers take down phone numbers for everyone they have spoken to, again, and also speak to Joey about the incident with Tommy Guinness. Just as they are about to leave, there is some commotion in the training centre. Mulligan and Carver look around to see Mark Strong confronting Matt Blast.

"What did you say about me!?" Mark is demanding of Matt, shoving him in the chest. Matt does not respond and just stares at Mark. There is a significant size difference between the two so Matt doesn't move when Strong shoves him. Eventually, Strong "pie-faces" Matt – shoves him in the face with the palm of his hand. Mulligan and Carver realise that this has escalated and walk swiftly towards the two. However, before they are able to get there, Matt Blast has hit Mark Strong with a right hook. Mark Strong is laying there, motionless.

Mulligan and Carver let out a sigh almost in unison. Mulligan crouches down beside the injured Mark Strong, checks his pulse and then calls for an ambulance on her radio. Meanwhile, Carver is speaking to Matt Blast, who seems a bit stunned at what he has just done.

"I'm going to have to ask you to stay standing there, Matt."

Matt doesn't respond, but also doesn't move from his spot. Joey der Verlierer and the two young trainees look on with their mouths agape. Danny Zaparcia tries to stage manage the situation with generally unhelpful results.

"Okay. Everyone back," Danny shouts, as if the room is packed. "Let the officers do their job."

The only people in the vicinity are the two young trainees, who are still in the ring and therefore quite far away from the situation.

Mulligan calls out to Joey, "can you get me a damp cloth?"

Joey snaps out of his shock for long enough to do as he's told, and within a few seconds brings over a damp dishcloth. Mulligan places the cloth on Mark's forehead. After a few seconds, Mark's eyes begin to flicker and the look of shock and stress on Matt Blast's face gives way to relief, as it does for the rest of the people in the room. Matt Blast himself begins to move and shuffle around on his feet for the first time in a while. Mulligan speaks in a loud, clear voice to Mark. He looks up at her and after a few moments, appears to be fully alert and sat down. Now that Mark Strong appears to be okay, Jake Carver begins to explain to Matt that he's going to have to arrest him and proceeds to read him his rights. Throughout the incident, Matt remains calm and listens to Carver, clearly still repeating what has just happened in his head.

Apparently, the punch that Matt Blast delivered to Mark Strong has taken the fight out of Mark, so even when he is back on his feet, Mark is focusing on recovering his bearings rather than confronting Matt. Shortly after Mark has got to his feet, the ambulance arrives and begin to check on Mark. Carver uses this opportunity to manoeuvre Matt Blast out of the building and into the back of the police car. The paramedics determine that Mark does not need to be taken to a hospital but advise him to stay somewhere where there is someone to look after him and to go to the A&E department if his symptoms worsen.

Chapter 8

Rite of Passage

"Guys," Huckle extends his vowels to try to force a sound of sincerity. "I really didn't know that she was under sixteen. I would never do something like that, if I had known. I have too much to lose."

Huckle is speaking to two male police officers, one apparently of Indian sub-continent descent and one who is white, both of average height. The white police officer sits forward in his chair, sighs and re-arranges some pieces of paper that are laid out in front of him on the desk between them.

"I wish that was true, Mr. Huckle – I really do. Unfortunately, we have chat logs from your victim's phone showing that you did, in fact, know that she was under the age of sixteen."

"Huckle says, 'how old are you, anyway?' to which Becky responds 'I'll be fifteen in a couple of months'. Huckle replies, 'niiiiice' with five "I"s. Does this sound familiar at all?"

Huckle turns to look at the man sat next to him, a skinny, balding middle-aged man, who firmly shakes his head in response to Huckle's gaze.

"No comment," Huckle responds to the police officer.

…

"Who's that sat with her?" Danny Zaparcia wonders as he and Huckle peak through the curtain at a teenage girl in the audience sat next to a middle-aged man.

"I think it's her Dad…" Huckle responds, with great disappointment and a forlorn expression.

Huckle returns to standing behind the curtain rather than peeking through it, "Agh! I can't believe she's brought her Dad with her!"

"She still looks good, though," Danny remarks, still peeking through the curtain at her. "I'd still try to hit that, if I was you."

"Don't worry. I'm still going to do it. Her Dad can fuck off."

Having done this sort of thing many times before, Huckle has a strategy in to the bag of exactly how he is going to deal with this problem. He quickly puts his mask and cape on and walks through the curtain. Several kids at once exclaim, "Look! It's Huckle!" before a chant of "Let's go Huckle! Let's go Huckle!" starts up, primarily amongst the younger members of the audience. Huckle spends around 5-10 minutes talking to some of the kids and posing for photos, slowly making his way up the steps to his true target: a certain girl, only slightly older than his regular fans.

Some of the kids follow Huckle around wherever he goes, talking to him, asking him questions, wrestling his leg and displaying other forms of rambunctious behaviour. Huckle makes his way to the teen girl he has had his eye on. The girl says something to her father, which Huckle cannot hear. Then, after continuously responding to the kids' shouts, introduces himself to the girl and her father.

"Good evening, el Padros!" he begins in his best attempt at a Mexican accent. "I am the one and only Huckle! How is the young lady, today?"

"Very well, thank you."

"And, this here must be your older brother!"

Her father pauses for a split second and looks up at Huckle, before smiling and saying, "Ha ha! Flattery will get you everywhere!"

Continuing his use of the fake Mexican accent, Huckle turns back around to the kids and calls out, "Who wants to come backstage and meet the wrestlers?"

Many of the kids shout in approval.

"Go ask your mamas and papas, and then come back to see me!" Huckle turns back around to the teen girl. "You too, young lady. If it is okay with your older brother, there!"

The girl's father nods and smiles, "Of course!"

Over the course of the next several minutes, Huckle, the girl and the kids slowly make their way back down the steps and through the curtain. Huckle does genuinely allow the children to meet many of the wrestlers, but as soon as he can, he either hands them off to the other wrestlers to look after or sends them back out to watch the show and cheer for him when he comes out.

"You know what to say, when I come out, right? You should shout 'Huckle! Huckle! Huckle!' Yes! Go out and have fun, now!"

Of course, Huckle pays extra attention to the teenage girl, introducing her with extra gusto to all of the wrestlers in the changing room, many of whom are polite to her, but are encased in an aura of awkwardness and dread. After many of them have been introduced to the girl, their gazes continue to follow the pair: not lustfully, but nervously. A serious expression crosses their faces, followed sometimes by long stares in to the distance. This is accompanied by a long period of silence as all of the wrestlers in the vicinity apparently mull over the same subject.

As the number of younger children gradually whittles down, Huckle settles in to sitting next to the teenage girl on chairs sitting next to each other. They are fairly cheap office chairs with stainless steel legs and fabric cushions attached to the seat and back. Huckle talks to the girl about all sorts of things in her life, from her hobbies and interests, to where she has seen him wrestle in the past, to her romantic relationships. He always wears a broad smile across his face, which the girl mimics without really noticing it. When Huckle smiles, she smiles. When Huckle laughs, she laughs. Meanwhile, not many of the other wrestlers in the changing rooms are able to hear what they're talking about, as the volume has increased since the initial shock of seeing the pair together, and the wrestlers are for the most part back to discussing their matches and talking about mundane and inconsequential things.

All of this changes when, around fifteen minutes into the meeting, Huckle invites the girl to grab his bum. Embarrassed but not protesting, she giggles and blushes before reaching out and grabbing it. At this point, a couple of the other wrestlers exit the room. Huckle then proceeds to remove his tights, as if he is going to change his clothes, even though he has not yet wrestled. This leaves him sitting there in just a thong with the girl noticeably struggling to maintain her gaze with his eyes, but repeatedly glancing at the bulge that is now so close to her line of vision. Nonetheless, it appears that this is what Huckle wants, as he sits there with his legs casually spread apart, continuing to converse with the girl.

It is at this point that Danny Zaparcia sneaks up behind him and whispers in his ear, "Do you mind if I have a quick word with you, Huckz?"

Huckle raises his eyebrows and looks around at Danny, sighing in mild frustration but apparently suspecting that this has something to do with the show that night. The wrestling show, that is, rather than the strip show that Huckle had been putting on for the girl. Huckle turns completely towards Zaparcia.

"Yeah?"

"This is a bit awkward, but I thought I would just tell you: I think that girl's underaged, dude. Does she have any ID on her that you can check?"

Huckle's head suddenly snapped up to face Danny as square-on as possible, his eyes widening with an intimidating intensity.

"Do you think I'm stupid, Danny? Do you really think I would do something like that with someone I knew to be under-aged? She's 18! We've already talked about it! Mind your own fucking business!"

Danny, a consummate coward, stands there, unable to move like a big, ugly rabbit in the headlights, eyes widened. As soon as he regains his bearings, he arches over and backs away, raising the palms of his hands up as if to demonstrate that he's unarmed.

"I'm sorry, I'm sorry! I didn't mean to upset you!"

"Yeah! Well, mind your own business, okay!?"

As if the shouting had suddenly triggered off a chain reaction, more shouting can then be heard from a couple of rooms away.

"Hey, guys! You can't be in here!" Joey der Verlierer shouts.

"Get the fuck out of here!" Sidney demands.

"We're looking for a wrestler called Huckle! He's a Paedophile! We're professional Paedophile hunters! Let us do our jobs!"

As soon as they had finished this diatribe, the owner of the loud, Scouse accent and two others enter the same room that Huckle is stood in, who is stood there with a look of both shock and anger stricken across his face.

"Are you Huckle!? Fred Funk!?"

"Yes! What the fuck do you want!?"

The scruffy, skinny scouse man backed up by two slightly bigger, bald men, fires back, whilst holding his mobile phone in front of him as if to defend himself with it as a weapon.

"We have evidence that you have been communicating with an underage girl in a sexual way and arranging to have sex with her. The police have been called. We suggest that you stay exactly where you are."

Whilst the scruffy man is saying this, the two bald men, who have been attempting to defend themselves and the scruffy man from being pushed out of the changing room, get in to a pushing match with a couple of the other wrestlers, who insist that they leave the changing rooms immediately.

"Hey! HEY!" calls the obnoxious scruffy man to the wrestlers. "I suggest you stop it! You're on live stream! Everything's being recorded!"

"Yeah?" Huckle screams in a high-pitched squeal. "Well, record this!"

Huckle marches up to the scruffy man and swings at his head with his fist. The man leans back and the punch only grazes him above his eye, but Huckle then grabs him by the scruff of his shirt and begins to throw uppercuts in to his face.

The teenage girl takes this opportunity to sneak out of the room through a different door.

The two bald men try to defend the scruffy man and tackle Huckle, but they are still in a shoving match with some of the other wrestlers. This leads to a big, ugly scene where Huckle is laying on the floor with the scruffy man still by his neck, trying to throw punches, whilst one of the bald men has tackled him to the ground and the wrestlers they have been in a shoving match with getting increasingly aggressive. Everyone is shouting orders, exclaiming anger and trying to gain control of the situation.

Suddenly, a huge burst of energy pushes through the crowd, and in enter the Whacko Bros., knocking everyone down in their way, including the wrestlers and one of the bald men. With them, is Mark Strong. The three of them grab the bald men and the scruffy man by the scruff of their necks and throw them in to a corner, before standing between them and Huckle. The three men are stood near the same door that the teenage girl exited by.

"Go on!" shouts the older of the Whacko Bros. "Fuck off!"

The three Liverpudlian men look like they have been struck by a tornado and are struggling to regain their bearings.

"Did I stutter!?" The older Whacko Bro. asks and takes a couple of aggressive steps towards the three. "Stand up and go through that door!"

"But...but..." the scruffy man stutters. "...my phone."

The Whacko Bro. sighs and looks around on the floor. "Where is it?" Mark Strong picks it up from the floor and hands it to him. The Whacko Bro. throws it at him and the scruffy man scrambles to pick it up.

"Right. There you go. Now, I'm only going to say this one more time. Fuck off!"

The three get to their feet, their eyes darting around as they try to reconcile their pride with their safety. But, after a couple of moments, the scruffy man feigns anger, pulls the door open violently and storms out of the room, with the two bald men following quietly behind. Once out of the door, they scamper away back into the public area.

Huckle sighs and lays back on the floor, exhausted. The Whacko Bros. and Mark Strong look upon Huckle, as if thinking of whether to say something or not.

"WHERE IS THAT BASTARD!?" another familiar voice rings out, this time even louder and more gruff. It is the father of the teenage girl. The Whacko Bros. and Mark Strong look up and see that they are being charged by a balding middle-aged man, his face reddened with rage. "THAT'S MY DAUGHTER HE'S MESSING AROUND WITH!"

The Whacko Bros. raise their hands up as if trying to reason with the man, but the man instead charges right past them, pushing into the left shoulder of the younger Whacko Bro. and looks towards the floor. Somehow, he seems to know exactly where Huckle is and has headed straight for him.

"IS THIS HIM!?" he screams, shouting at Huckle who is laying on the floor, his knees now bent, his head raised and the palms of his hands raised in a defensive position. Huckle's eyes widen in fear and he stammers as he tries to say something. This appears to confirm in the man's mind that this truly is the man who has been trying to seduce his underaged daughter. He quickly jumps down and mounts Huckle, before raining down a series of hard, bear-like swipes to either side of Huckle's head. He shouts out a word of a sentence after each one.

"DON'T! MESS! AROUND! WITH! YOUNG! GIRLS! YOU! FREAK!"

Huckle has his arms up around his head, trying desperately to defend himself. The man's punches sometimes hit his arms and sometimes hit the side of his head. Before he is able to do too much damage, the Whacko Bros., Mark Strong and Matt Blast hook his arms and begin to pull him away. As he is being pulled away, he continues to blurt things out.

"No! That bastard! Let me go!"

He also manages to land a hard stomp to the groin of Huckle. Matt Blast gets in front of the man, wraps his arms around his waist and pushes him as if trying to push a broken-down car down the road. Over the course of the next couple of minutes, the four manage to drag the man out of the changing room, before a couple of the wrestlers continue to speak to the man at the entrance of the changing room and calm him down, which involves the frequent repeating of the phrase, "wait for the police to get here."

Huckle remains laying on the ground, writhing around. He lets out an even bigger sigh than before. Danny Zaparcia peaks over at him.

"Are you okay, Hux?"

Another big sigh and a pause.

"Not really, Danny…" a defeated Huckle says with a breathy, exhausted voice.

There is a pause in which everyone in the vicinity stands in silence and stares at Huckle as he lays on the floor, licking his wounds. Danny Zaparcia, in particular, gives a long stare in the general direction of Huckle with his mouth agape. Danny's lips quiver a bit as if he is about to say something, but he doesn't. He then looks away, lowers his head and then shouts out towards the floor, "Well, the police will look after you when they get here, anyway."

The silence somehow seems to get even more silent, as no-one – not Huckle, nor anyone in the room or even Zaparcia himself – could have predicted that Zaparcia would have developed a spine strong enough to say what he really felt about "Hux". However, given the position of extreme weakness that Huckle is in, having been attacked and laying there exhausted and waiting for the police to arrive in order to arrest him, Danny was able to pluck up the courage long enough to speak the unutterable.

Huckle pushes himself up with his hands and sits there, dazed. In response to Danny, he says, "Shut up, Danny, you fucking loser."

Danny, spurred on by everyone's delight in beating up Huckle, considers whether to just go over and continue the beating on Huckle. Instead, Danny says, "No, Hux. You're the loser, now."

Danny, his body full of adrenaline, heads for the door in front of him, clumsily and hastily opening it, worried that he might spoil his moment of victory. His moment of using Huckle as a symbol of Danny Zaparcia's failure and standing up to it.

Indeed – the police do arrive and perform their duties. They clear the area and calm everyone down, arrest Huckle, tend to his injuries, take statements from everyone in the vicinity, and then place Huckle in the back of a police car. At this point, Huckle is resigned to his fate and looking defeated, his shoulders sagging, his face drooped, and his eyes engaged in a distant stare outside of the window. A few of the wrestlers come out to see him in the police car. But they do not smile or mock him, nor does he attempt to provoke them. They simply watch him as he meets his fate, like a lamb going to the slaughter or a murderer in Alabama who has just been sentenced to death. The scene has a ceremonial feel to it: a feeling of something that must be done: the justice finally served to one of British wrestling's biggest embarrassments.

...

One of the biggest misogynistic losers in wrestling has just been arrested. Good riddance, Huckle.

- Lizzie Austin

Yes! The day has finally come! Now, everyone will see Huckle for the lowlife that he really is!

- Tommy Guinness

These exclamations were followed up by both by long, detailed stories of what had actually happened, right in front of them. Whilst Lizzie Austin lectured on the importance of this for women within professional wrestling, Tommy Guinness expressed excitement and amusement that someone who was consistently "an arsehole" to so many people for so many years had been arrested and got what was coming to him.

Their messages were quickly followed by many other people finally feeling free to pile on with their own stories of Huckle. Stories of him having sex with underaged girls, of being "an arsehole" to people, of generally being a weird, unpleasant man, and so forth. Some of these stories were years old. Maybe the writers had told them before but had been ignored. Maybe they were just trying not to step on eggshells so as to not upset him and have opportunities taken from them by Huckle's group of sycophants.

Speaking of sycophants, the first reaction of many was to defend Huckle and assume that he must be innocent. Because, if there's ever any defence against being a perverted criminal, it's having entertained people who are then unwilling to let go of those feelings to accept the reality of the individual. Admittedly, some of the stories that came out about Huckle were probably false, but many of them were also likely true. The dam had burst, and a waterfall of hatred and resentment had come gushing out to shower the now drowned reputation of Huckle.

Nonetheless, Sidney remained savvy to the ways of the internet. He knew that his relationship with Huckle – involving in itself plenty of sycophancy – would reflect poorly on him. Therefore, he began immediately arguing with the people who had bad things to say about Huckle and insisted that everyone should wait for the legal proceedings to play out. But the internet was busy having their own court and a decision was quickly made: Huckle's career was over. Deals that he had, he was released from. Many, many promoters, some who hadn't ever booked him in the first place, provided statements that said that they would never book him. Nonetheless, Sidney pressed on and made a statement on his company's website:

As many of you will be aware by now, the professional wrestler known as Huckle (real name: Fred Funk) has today been arrested. This took place during one of my shows, taking place in Barnsley.

Many of us have known Fred for many years, now, and he has brought joy to a lot of us through his performances and through his personality: always wanting to meet fans and make them happy, especially younger fans. So, I think we owe it to him to wait until the criminal proceedings have played out to see whether or not he is truly guilty of what he is being accused of.

In the meantime, please refrain from messaging his family and friends about this. They will be having a hard enough time as it is.

Thank you.

Sidney

All of this occurred over such a short period of time, and so suddenly, that the show was still going on when Sidney provided that statement. But, as dramatic as the scene had been, it was about to become all the more dramatic in around 45 minutes from then.

But, first, for a public announcement from the Yorkshire Anti-Nonce Network, as they called themselves. Returning to the changing rooms, as everyone was preoccupied by the presence of the police and had quietened down due to a combination of sharing what had happened on social media and simply being exhausted by the situation, the scruffy man and the two bald men returned to the changing room. They were seemingly reinvigorated by being backed up by the police and had completely forgotten about the scruffy one getting beaten up only a few minutes prior. Apparently on a whim, the scruffy one strutted around the changing rooms, shouting out a speech of hatred for professional wrestling.

"Professional wrestling has a big problem with paedophilia! Not only that, but professional wrestling has a big problem with a lot of different people! Black people, gay people, women! You see yourselves as these big stars who are untouchable and everyone else has to look up to you and do your bidding!"

With smirks on their faces, the bald men proceed to follow the scruffy man around as he continues his speech.

"Well, guess what: tonight, you're wrestling in front of a hundred people in some social club! You're nobodies! You always will be nobodieeeeeeeees..!"

The scruffy one's speech was suddenly brought to an end through the combined force of Matt Blast, Mark Strong and the Whacko Bros., the older one of whom grabbed the scruffy one by the scruff of the neck, partially choking him, and marched him back towards the curtain. All three of the men were rushed outside and given parting kicks, to the mid-section, to the head, to the rear end, as they left.

Sidney's eyes lit up with excitement as he saw Mark Strong handle the self-proclaimed paedophile hunters. He would once again approach Mark Strong, whilst he knew that Tommy Guinness was in the other changing room, to once again encourage him to take some liberties with Guinness.

"Okay. I'll handle it," Mark said, still fired up from the earlier scene. "I said I'll handle it, so I'll handle it."

Sidney's face lit up. Despite the fact that he had just been found to be employing and defending a paedophile, that the police were investigating his show and that several of his acquaintances were sleeping with his wife, he relished the idea that the night would feature a singular shining moment which he could hold on to. A moment which would give him a sense of power and control of his situation, something he had lacked for so long.

Sidney had got into promoting wrestling because he had always been a fan of professional wrestling, but did not have the ability or commitment to become good at it himself. Noticing how fellow trainees would treat promoters to get bookings, he decided that he wanted some of that for himself. He didn't care whether it was false respect or real respect. He just wanted the power to make people treat him in that way. Unfortunately, that hadn't always gone according to plan. As he tried to build his wrestling promotion, he under-estimated the amount of work he would have to do to attract an audience to his events. Many of his early events drew very low numbers and cost him a lot of money, which impacted upon how many people would contact him to beg him for bookings.

Eventually, others who had been around wrestling for some time – such as Mark Strong, the Whacko Bros., etc. – basically took on a lot of the load and he was gradually able to improve the size of his audiences. But, the damage to his reputation had been done. On top of this, everyone knew about the situation with his wife and routinely mocked him about it behind his back, and sometimes in front of him. People knew that he would try to get other people's shows cancelled. The only people who would show him the respect he craved so much were other people such as himself – those who did not have the ability or commitment to succeed on a higher level and would therefore try to blag their way on to any shows that they possibly could. These people felt very strongly about Sidney because he was the only one, in their minds, who had ever "given them a chance". Sidney liked these people very much and would continue to book them, not for their ability, but because of how they made him feel about himself.

Chapter 9

The Point of the Sword

Once Huckle had been questioned for a couple of hours by the officers who arrested him, the interview is concluded and it is explained to Huckle that two other police officers wished to speak to him regarding the Michael Ali incident that occurred on the same night. The door to the interview room opens and in walk Jane Mulligan and Jake Carver. All four officers smile at each other, cordially, and then Mulligan and Carver calmly sit down opposite Huckle.

"As the officers you have just spoken to may have already explained to you," Mulligan began. "We would like to ask you a few questions regarding an incident that occurred last night at the same venue as, uh, the incident that you were involved in. Do you know what I'm talking about?"

A dejected, downtrodden Huckle, slouching in his chair, does not bother to look up at Mulligan or Carver, and replies simply and quietly, "Yeah. Someone told me about it on the phone. About Michael."

Mulligan nods.

"That's right. So, we're just going to re-set the recorder here and then we'll ask you a few questions about that."

Mulligan does as she says, before introducing the people in the room and giving the time and date of the interview for the benefit of the recording.

"Okay, Mr. Funk. How well do you know Sidney and Michael Ali?"

Funk sits up in his chair, slightly.

"I have met Michael. I don't know much about him. I know that he's…quite serious about his religion."

"And, Sidney?"

"Sidney, I have worked on some of his shows over the past couple of years. I don't really like him as a person, so I don't spend much personal time with him. I think he likes to think that we're friends, though."

"How have you got that impression?" Carver interjects.

"Um…he'll just post a lot on social media of photos of me and him together. He does that with a few people. I guess he wants to be popular."

"Well…" Carver continues. "…the reason that we want to talk to you, today, is because we feel that you could perhaps provide some background to Sidney's recent situation. I understand that, given your own circumstances, you might not be in…the best of spirits, shall we say, but I think it probably can't hurt to tell us what you know about Sidney's situation."

Silence prevails for a few seconds, before Funk nods gently. Carver and Mulligan wait for a clearer agreement.

"Sure. I'll tell you what I know."

"Great."

"The first thing we want to know, and this might sound strange: are you familiar with Sidney's situation with his wife? Their lifestyle?" Mulligan enquires.

Huckle fidgets. "I only know that they have an open relationship. But no-one wants to sleep with him. So, that basically means that everyone sleeps with his wife, but not him. He seems pretty bitter about that."

"Anyone from within wrestling?"

"Yeah…Tommy Guinness is the current one, I think."

"And, you say that Sidney has struggled to deal with this?"

"Yeah. He seems to. He holds grudges against everyone who sleeps with his wife. He tries to get them fired from their jobs. If they're in wrestling, he tries to blackball them."

"Why has he kept booking Tom, then?"

"I think it's because his wife likes him and they're…" Huckle uses air quotes. "…'friends'. So, if Sidney stops booking him and she finds out why this is, then there's going to be trouble with his wife. He doesn't want to lose her: I think that's why he had this idea to begin with. They met over ten years ago and he's become gradually more depressed, drunk, fat and so on as time went on, and I think his wife was thinking of getting a divorce. So, he came up with this. It hasn't worked, though. He's still miserable."

"Okay," Mulligan pauses as she finishes noting down what Huckle has said. "Thank you. Have you noticed Sidney and Michael spending a lot of time, together, recently?"

"I have. Sidney often takes him to dinner and to bars. At first, I thought they were having a gay relationship. But then, when you consider what Michael thinks of homosexuals, that seems pretty unlikely."

"Would you speculate as to whether you think Sidney had anything to do with planning this event that happened, last night, with Michael?"

"It wouldn't surprise me…wait – you mean, Michael's attack, right?"

"Yes."

"Yeah. I don't think it would surprise me. Sidney has been very unstable for quite a long time, now, so I wouldn't put anything off the table."

Carver looks down at the desk for a moment, considering how he will word his next question. "We have heard from some of the other wrestlers on the show that they heard Michael saying some quite extremist things. And, you yourself have also said that you heard him saying these things…"

"Yeah."

Carver sighs. "But no-one has thought to report this to the police, it seems. Why is that? Is there some sort of code of silence over things like this amongst wrestlers?"

"I don't know whether there's a code of silence. But, if someone complained to Sidney that Michael was crazy, given how much they see of each other, it would probably hurt them."

"But, what about the police? You could always report it anonymously to the police."

"Yes. But…yeah…I guess, in wrestling, it is kind of a thing to try to resolve things amongst ourselves rather than going to the police."

There is an awkward silence that follows this, as all three participants in the conversation's minds go to Huckle's own crimes and the parallels with Michael Ali. All three try to mask that they're thinking about that by shuffling in their seats and not making eye contact.

…

The room is filled with noise of many different conversations taking place at the same time. It is a smorgasbord of different emotions. Happiness, excitement, boredom, lethargy. Some conversations are carried out in hushed voices with the participants' heads lowered closer to the table that sits between them. Others bellow out as if there is no-one else in the room. The room is warm from the full house of people contained within, all breathing carbon dioxide into the air, slowly increasing the temperature. Whilst there is no air conditioning to balance out the temperature, there are ceiling fans which cool down the areas immediately below them. The ceiling-to-floor windows covering seemingly the entire exterior of the building are frosted up from condensation, only the glow of the streetlights piercing through them.

In one of the booths of this New York Italian family restaurant chain, sits a scruffy man with an equally scruffy beard, a football shirt and short dark hair. Across the table from him sits a young Bangladeshi man with black hair and intense eyes. It appears that the scruffy man he is speaking to is doing most of the talking.

"What most people don't realise, these days, is it isn't about how many moves you can do, but whether you have that connection with the audience. That's why my promotion is doing so well, at the moment. The videos that we put out there really extend our reach to a lot of people and make people more interested in the show than they otherwise would have. That translates in to merchandise sales. I bet we have more merchandise sales than anyone else in the UK, at least in the north of England. Because, people actually care about the characters."

The Bangladeshi man just stares at the man he is speaking to, politely nodding in parts whilst sipping on a Diet Coke.

"A lot of people criticise me for putting myself on my own shows. But, I've gotta be honest, I have better mic' skills than almost anyone else in the country, right now. I make people hate me and want to pay money for people to beat me up. That's what it's all about, after all. Most of the people who criticise me couldn't draw flies to a donkey turd. That's what I think you need to work on. I think we need to start working on your character. I can speak for you, be your mouthpiece, to begin with. But, we need to build a character around you that will make the audience either love you and want to pay money to see you, or hate you and make people want to pay money to see you get beaten up."

At this point, the young man's eyes are beginning to glaze over, as he has heard this same spiel in exactly these terms from this exact same man many times. In fact, every time they come here, he gives him this spiel. But Michael just lets him do it as he doesn't want to upset him and it would be more trouble than it's worth to try to change the subject.

Sidney, having finally noticed that Michael has not said anything for a good twenty minutes, pauses. First, he wonders why Michael hasn't spoken for so long, then realises that it's because he's been speaking for the entire time and then, finally – with a half-puzzled, half-sympathetic expression on his face – considers how to reintegrate Michael back in to the conversation. It is at this moment that Sidney finally recalls what he wanted to speak to Michael about: the reason he brought Michael to this New York Italian family restaurant, in the first place.

"Michael…" Sidney begins in an inquisitive voice, cupping his left hand in his right hand. "I was just wondering whether you could tell me more about your religion and how you see the world. Y'know – that sort of thing?"

Michael's interest is suddenly aroused. He sits up in his seat and pushes the Diet Coke to the side, slightly.

"What exactly would you like to know?"

Sidney licks his upper lip and then retracts it back into his mouth, whilst thinking about his next words. Expressing himself with his arms and hands as well as his mouth, he continues, "I suppose, what I want to know is..." He holds out his hands as if holding a ball. "...how do you see the world and how do you think it SHOULD be?"

"I think it's a mess." Michael dives right in.

"Uh-huh."

"I think the governments of the USA, the UK, NATO and all the rest of them have been taking part in trying to kill off the Muslim way of life, to kill our people – all for the sake of oil. I think we need to remember what it says in the Qur'an – remember the ways of Mohammed – and that is to spread the word of Mohammed at the point of the sword. By force. To convert the world to Islam. That is the only way. If we don't do this, then the West is going to continue to walk all over us and kill our people. It has been a genocide and we can't afford to be ignorant, any longer. If anyone's going to commit genocide, it needs to be us. Because, we have Allah on our side. Whether it is through military action or becoming a martyr – we must be prepared to die and to kill the infidels in order to spread the word of Mohammed and of Allah!"

Michael's voice has steadily crept up through the duration of his monologue, to the point where several people in the vicinity are looking up from their meals and their conversations and staring at him.

"Okay…" Sidney interjects, nodding and stretching out his hand to try to calm down Michael.

"Don't try to calm me down! This has been going on for too long!"

Michael has stood up from his seat and his hunched over the table, his index finger pointed at Sidney.

"Since the Spanish Inquisitions, the West have victimised Muslims!"

"Okay, okay. I'm sorry. I'm sorry," Sidney says, hastily, cringing awkwardly and looking around at the several tables around him where everyone has stopped their conversations to watch the scene that is unfolding.

"It's not right!"

Michael sits down, aggressively, as if he is attempting to push himself through the seat. "Well? Is it!?"

"No. Not at all. In fact…"

Sidney looks around him to make sure that most of the people watching can't hear him. Just to make sure, he lowers his voice slightly and leans over the table.

"That's the reason that I wanted to talk to you about it. Erm…just one more thing I would like to ask you. What are your thoughts on the Conservative Party, at the moment?"

Having not yet calmed down completely, Michael starts off his response, immediately and firmly.

"They've always been hateful, Islamophobic bastards!"

Some customers from the other tables look around at him, again, and say something about the scene between themselves, but it is inaudible to Sidney.

"Right. Well, um…On this weekend's show, we're going to be having the Conservative Party mayor in attendance…"

Michael's eyes widen in indignation and he opens his mouth to speak, but Sidney stretches out his hand again.

"…Just…let me finish. The mayor THINKS he's here to support our work for the cancer charity we're raising money for. But I have another idea, and it involves you."

"Oh?"

"Yes. I think this might be your opportunity – to make a stand and become a martyr. I know you've told me about how you've managed to put together that homemade bomb of yours. Well, this could be the time for you to use it. And, become a martyr. To serve Allah."

Suddenly, the gravity of the situation appears to have rested on Michael's shoulders, and Michael looks back at Sidney with a sombre expression.

"I can set everything up to give you the perfect opportunity to do it. You'll just need to walk out there and trigger your bomb."

Sidney pauses to allow Michael to respond, who also pauses and continues to stare at Sidney as he thinks through the proposition.

"I don't know. I was kind of planning to kill John Cleese."

A flash of confusion and bemusement crosses Sidney's face, but he quickly forces it away, "John Cleese? John Cleese is an old man. He will be dying, soon, anyway."

"How old is the mayor?"

"Forty-four. So, he's got thirty or forty years of Islamophobia left in him. He couldn't even end up in the Cabinet, or perhaps be the Prime Minister."

Michael nods to himself, apparently content with this argument. He looks up to Sidney, as if he were a wise teacher.

"But, why do YOU want the mayor dead?" he asks.

"Well, I don't like the Tories, either. They're not only Islamophobic, but they're racist, homophobic and they're intolerant of alternative lifestyles..."

Considering his own homophobic views, Michael raises his eyebrows to Sidney's explanation.

"...as you may know, I have an alternative lifestyle, and so I want to send a message. Also, my wife will be in attendance...and she needs to die, too."

"So, you want to kill both the mayor and your wife?"

"Yeah. I'll set it up so it's perfect. You won't need to worry about it. I'll take care of it and get the perfect opportunity."

Michael sits in silence for a bit longer, looks towards the table, inhales deeply, looks out of the window as if to see his fate emerging over the horizon and finally sits up in his seat.

"Okay. I'll see what I can do."

"I don't need you to see, Michael. If I'm going to set this up, I need you to do it. This is our one opportunity."

Michael tilts his head to the left, and lets his mouth open a bit. "Okay. Let's do it."

"That's great, Michael. You're going to have your virgins and there'll be one less whore in the world."

Sidney reaches his hand out to Michael, who shakes it. Sidney then wraps his left hand around the back of Michael's hand and squeezes it, softly.

Chapter 10

Bald Bill

This industry just lost two of the worst womanising, misogynistic creeps there are going. And one crazy terrorist. It is a good day for the world. How anyone could have let a terrorist be around their shows for so long is unthinkable. Unless you remember that it was Sidney whose shows it was in the first place. I wouldn't be surprised if Sidney was involved in this, as well.

- Lizzie Austin

This is why you can't just have anyone promoting shows. Because, they book people like Michael Ali and think they're all powerful and can do whatever they want.

- Dr. Steel

A very dire day for the industry. How could anyone let this sort of thing happen? A Paedophile, a terrorist and whatever Sidney is, all in one promotion. This cannot be allowed to happen again.

- 'The Thunder' Mike Brown

Shortly after posting these messages, following the sycophancy that immediately followed from their friends and the few fans that they had, was a stream of conversations all centred around the same subject.

If you knew about it for so long, why didn't you tell the police?

Oh, look. Some strawbs want to pretend to be heroes, even though they let it happen for so long and didn't do anything about it. Idiots.

If you knew what these people were really like and never did anything about it, you're part of the problem.

I wouldn't be surprised if 'Thunder' Mike Brown was involved in this in some way. He's a creep, himself.

The responses from Lizzie Austin, Brown and Steel were to be anticipated: all three played the victim and claimed to be the object of online harassment.

And, here we go again. A woman has an opinion on something in wrestling, and immediately, she is threatened and harassed by everyone online. Get a life. Really.

- Lizzie Austin

It's easy to criticise people when you're not there in that situation. Don't be cowards. Don't harass people online. You wouldn't have been any different.

- Dr. Steel

How dare you accuse me of somehow being involved in this!? I've never done anything even resembling this. I think you're just accusing me because of my skin colour, to be honest. The next person I see accusing me of this, I'm reporting to the police.

- 'The Thunder' Mike Brown

The backlash continued with many questioning why they hadn't been as angry and willing to go to the police when they had a paedophile and a terrorist getting to work right next to them for so long.

...

This is one of the most dysfunctional teams of any kind that I've ever been a part of, thinks Mike Brown. Not just for a "locker room" full of wrestlers, but on any cricket or rugby team he's ever been on, on any team he's ever been put on at work as a lab technician, or any team that he was forced to be a part of at school. There are just so many insane, malevolent, selfish people on this team than anywhere else that he's ever experienced. After speaking to the mentally challenged Whacko Bros., then speaking to the renowned paedophile Huckle, and having spent the past twenty minutes on the receiving end of a rant about how the Western world is exterminating Muslims, Brown staggers in a dazed state towards Sidney, the person who has recruited all of these lunatics, to ask him what he wants him to do that evening.

Sidney is sat on a bar chair, next to a bar table that has been set up on the stage, where he has some pieces of paper in front of him which he is marking with a permanent marker. Brown walks up the wooden steps to the stage and over to Sidney, seeing that he is still working on the match card for that day's show. Sidney looks up as he sees Brown coming towards him, glances back down at the paper in front of him, and then back up at Brown with a warm smile on his face which indicates that he had been wanting to speak to Brown.

"Alright?" Brown greets Sidney. "Do you know what you want me to do tonight, yet?"

Sidney pushes himself up with the table to get to his feet and walks calmly over to Brown.

"Yeah. I'm going to team you with Matt Blast against Joey and Steel. With you going over."

Brown nods, "Cool."

Then, in a quieter voice, Sidney leans into Brown and says, "there's something that I would like to speak to you about in private, if that's okay."

Detecting surprise in Brown's eyes, Sidney quickly follows up, "It's nothing that you've done wrong. I would just like to pick your brains about something."

Brown opens up his arms and the palms of his hands.

"Sure."

Brown then follows Sidney back down the wooden steps, out of the door of the room and in to a secluded part of the corridor, whilst wondering what it is that Sidney could possibly want to "pick [his] brains" about.

Sidney looks around them to make sure they're alone. A young wrestler walks from the toilet to the concert room and Sidney watches him until the wrestler is inside the concert room before he looks back at Brown. His eyes dart around for a moment, as he considers how to word what he is about to say.

"I understand that it might be strange that I am asking you this, as we have only just met."

Brown recoils his head and his eyes widen. Sidney notices this.

"No, no – it's nothing like that," Sidney lets out a snort of laughter. He pushes his lips together and then opens them again in an awkward, twisting motion. "It's about…my relationship with my wife…"

Brown sees where this is going and steps in, pre-emptively.

"Look, Sidney – I would like to help you out, but I'm really not into that kind of thing?"

Sidney's eyebrows furrow, "what kind of thing?"

"You know…You were looking at me, and you thought to yourself, there's a handsome, muscular black man. He'll look great fucking my wife. But, I don't do that sort of thing. I'm sorry."

Unsure whether Brown is being serious, Sidney lets out a second snort of laughter, quickly followed up by a concerned gaze. He then adopts a broad smile and says, "Oh. No, no! That's not what I was thinking!"

Brown's face remains serious. Sidney continues.

"It's just that I've had a problem with my relationship with my wife and I'm looking for some help…"

"Oh. Okay! I wasn't sure. You wouldn't believe how many times I've been asked to do that," Brown laughs.

"Have you ever taken anyone up on it, though?" Sidney jokes.

"…what?" Brown's expression has changed to a combination of confusion and insulted. "…no…why would I..?"

"I – I'm just kidding."

Brown takes a deep breath.

"Look, I'm probably not the best person to be asking for relationship advice," Brown continues. "I've just split up with my girlfriend, so…I'm not very good at choosing women who aren't crazy, y'know?"

"Oh. It's nothing like that. Erm…well, I might as well just tell you what it is. I have been having some problems with my wife, with our relationship…"

Sidney opens his arms out, impetuously, then goes back to a more conservative stance.

"...She's been screwing around with other men."

"O-kay..."

"And, this is a problem for me, because it...just isn't right."

Sidney stares off into the distance, thinking about what he wants to say, as Brown continues to wonder what he is being roped in to. Sidney once again leans in to Brown and lowers his voice, almost to a whisper.

"I need to get rid of her."

Brown hopes Sidney doesn't mean what he thinks he means.

"You mean, you want to get a divorce?"

"No..." Sidney draws back and looks at him, and for a moment reconsiders whether he should say this to Brown.

"I mean...I need to...GET RID...of her..."

Brown frowns.

"I hope you're not saying what I think you're saying."

"Why not? What's the problem?"

"I think you're saying that you want to kill your wife."

Sidney's heart pounds against his chest, as he realises this is the moment at which he is becoming completely vulnerable.

"That IS what I mean."

Brown's face contorts into a combination of confusion, anger and disgust.

"No..." he sighs. "...you don't want to do that..."

Realising that Brown is likely going to want to get out of his system how all this makes him feel, Sidney stays silent and lets Brown continue.

"...You don't want to do that. And, why did you ask ME about this? What can I do? Are you asking me to find someone to kill her? Why would I know something about that? Because, I'm black!?"

"No. I just thought..."

"Look. I work in a science lab, doing a really tedious, white collar job. I have never been on the streets. Apart from some weed in university, I've never even touched drugs. How exactly do you think I could help you..."

he begins to whisper shout. "...to kill your wife? And, even if I could, why would I want to? Look on the deep web or something. I don't know anything about this sort of thing. I don't even want anything to do with it. Keep me out of it. I don't want anyone to know that I talked to you about this."

"Oh, no-one will. Don't worry," Sidney, now visibly sweating, reassures Brown. "This isn't something I'm going to talk to just anyone about for obvious reasons. Look – I can't just go on the dark web: most of the ads for hitmen are undercover security agents."

"So, now, it's my problem!?"

"No. I'm not going to tell anyone that we had this conversation..."

"You better not."

"...I just thought I would ask you for some advice..."

"Why? Because I'm black?"

"No. I...I heard that it was something that you could probably help me with."

"Who told you that?"

"I don't want you to be getting angry at him..."

"No. I just want to know. Who told you that I could help you with this?"

"...Bald Bill."

"Bald Bill!? Bald Bill from Doncaster?"

"No. Nottingham Bald Bill."

"NOTTINGHAM Bald Bill!? Why did you ask Nottingham Bald Bill about this!?"

"Well, he approached me for a booking and we got talking..." Sidney cuts himself off and sighs. "Mike...I REALLY need your help with this. I don't think this can be resolved any other way. I just thought that, if you knew anyone, you would be able to suggest them and then we could forget that this conversation ever happened..."

As he is beginning to tune out to Sidney's begging, Mike suddenly has an idea flash in his mind. Not knowing or caring what Sidney is ranting about at that moment, Mike says, "I know who you can ask."

"What..? Really? Who?"

"Michael Ali."

Sidney's eyes narrow. "Is he a hitman?"

"I don't know. But, he's damn sure a jihadi in the making. If you can make it worth his while, if you can make it look like he's standing up to…'the tyranny of the West'…I'm sure he would help you."

As Sidney stood there, considering it, Mike continued, "I'm done with this conversation, now."

Mike walks off with many emotions running through his head. Relieved that he was finally able to get Sidney to shut up and leave him alone, but worried that he might have just been involved in something very serious. But, most of all, the over-arching emotions are bemusement, confusion and a rising sense of puzzlement over why he was in professional wrestling, if everyone was as insane as this. Finally, he thinks that it would make a good chapter in his autobiography when he eventually makes it big.

…

"Good afternoon. South Yorkshire Police."

"Yes. Hello. I believe you're investigating a murder that took place at West Duke Working Men's Club in Barnsley."

"Do you have information that you would like to share?"

"I do. I work at West Duke and, um, I think I have witnessed something that could be helpful to you."

"Okay. I'm happy to hear what it is you've witnessed."

"So, my Uncle who runs the pub wanted me to speak to the guy running the show to ask him something. I went into the main hall and couldn't find him, so I looked around for him. And, I went into the corridor. At the end of the corridor, there was Sidney and a black man, arguing over something. I thought I would stand around the corner and wait until they had finished before I spoke to Sidney. Well, I overheard what they were talking about. Sidney was asking Mike Brown if he knew anyone that he could hire to kill his wife."

"Sidney's wife?"

"Yeah."

"What did the black man say in response? Did he suggest someone?"

"Yeah. He suggested Michael Ali. I remember the name because it reminded me of Muhammed Ali."

"Okay. Do you have any idea what this black man's name was?"

"I'm pretty sure, but not certain, that I heard the promoter call him Mike. But he was the only black man there, I think, so if you look in to it, I think it will be pretty easy to figure out who it was."

"Could you give me a description of this man?"

"Sure. He was..."

...

"Good shot, Mike," a gentile man in his sixties commends, as he politely applauds his opponent.

That WAS a good shot, Mike thinks to himself. It feels good to be playing so well in front of the boss, like this. As his boss, Duncan, takes his time selecting the club he wants to use, Mike takes the opportunity to soak in his surroundings. The wind gently blowing through the leaves on the trees, the blue sky decorated with white fluffy clouds, the well-kept golfing greens, the horizon of Sheffield city centre in the distance, and not to mention, the company he is keeping. Mike takes a moment to appreciate that his life isn't half bad, after all.

"I think I'll go for the seven-iron for this one," Duncan smiles. Mike nods.

Duncan swings and hits the ball on to the green. But it rolls past the hole, and keeps rolling, until it is on the edge of the green.

"Argh," Duncan exclaims in dissatisfaction.

"It's not too far away. Just on the edge. You can recover."

At that moment, Mike sees something in the corner of his eye. Something out of place. A dark blur. He looks up to it and sees two figures walking down the green towards them. He then identifies their reflective clothing and unusual hats, symbols of police officers. Duncan, having seen the expression on Mike's face, follows his gaze over to the pair of police officers. For a moment, they both stare and simply watch the officers make their way down towards them, walking swiftly. Mike's stomach sinks. Are they after him? What could it be about? Is there some violent person who has been hiding on the golf course?

"What have you done?" Duncan jokes, smiling at Mike.

"Nothing, as far as I can remember."

But that wasn't true. As Mike had been rapidly searching his memories for things he had possibly done wrong, his mind was split between two possibilities: the contents of THAT FILE on his computer, and the conversation he had had with Sidney the week before. His heart sank. Maybe they aren't walking towards him. Maybe they are going to walk past. Mike tries to assess whether their trajectory means that they are going to walk past, but it has become clear that they are walking straight towards himself and Duncan. As they draw ever closer, Mike transitions from a feeling of dread to a determination to greet and communicate with the police officers. If he is going to be arrested in front of his boss and have his life thrown into disarray, then that is what is going to happen and there is nothing he can do about it. Eventually, the officers walk on to the green and finally greet the pair. They are both male, one a short Pakistani man and the other a taller Caucasian man. The Caucasian man addresses them.

"Good afternoon, gentleman. Is either of you, Mike Brown?"

Duncan meekly gestures up to Mike.

"That would be me," Mike confirms.

"Apologies for interrupting. Were you having a family game of golf?"

"No," Mike smiles. "He's my boss. Duncan Faustein."

"Ah. I see. Do you mind if we have a private word with you, Mike? We need to speak to you about an incident that occurred, recently, in Barnsley."

"Not at all."

Mike and Duncan arrange to meet up back at the clubhouse and then Mike follows the police officers to just beyond the tree line of the course.

"Okay. Thank you for your co-operation, Mr. Brown. There have been accusations made against you regarding aiding and abetting an attempted murder. Therefore, I'm going to have to place you under arrest so that we may question you and keep you in custody until the matter is resolved."

Mike can feel his heart pounding against his chest.

"If you could just put your arms out in front of you for me, please."

Mike follows the request and the police officer places handcuffs on his wrists.

"Mike Brown, I am placing you under arrest for suspicion of aiding and abetting an attempted murder. You do not have to say anything. But anything you do say may be taken in evidence in a court of law. Do you understand?"

"...yes."

Chapter 11

Kaboom

Jane Mulligan, Jake Carver and Sidney once again find themselves sitting on opposite sides of a rectangular table in a small room painted faded brilliant white with a voice recorder recording everything they say. Sidney still has the same solicitor sat next to him, looking tired as always.

Sidney is far more relaxed than he usually is, making friendly conversation with the two officers and even smiling.

"How have you been today, officers?"

Jane looks over to Jake, a bit puzzled, before responding, "Not bad, thank you. Just returned from lunch."

Sidney nods, "And what did you have for lunch?"

"I had a pasta salad and an apple."

"And I had a BLT," continues Jake, not entirely sure whether the conversation is appropriate.

"Ah. Lovely. The jail gave me a ham sandwich and a cup of tea. It was quite nice."

"That's good," Mulligan smiles. "You seem like you're in a good mood, today."

"Well, I think you're beginning to understand that I couldn't be involved in this, so I'm looking forward to going home and seeing my wife and friends, again."

Mulligan's eyebrows raise. "Well, we'll see what happens. We do have some things which we would like to go over with you."

"Sure. Go ahead."

"Thank you. When we last spoke, it was to confirm that Mike Brown's testimony did indeed corroborate with your own, that neither of you had any involvement or prior knowledge with Michael Ali's plan."

"That's right."

"You said that, whilst you two did have a conversation in the corridor that day, your conversation was about your plans for Brown, and that you were joking about your wife, and that this was probably misinterpreted by the witness who saw you two having your conversation."

"That's right."

"Mike agreed with this. And then, we told you about the results of our conversation with him."

"Correct," Sidney smiles and nods.

"Well, we wanted to cross-check what both of you had said, just to make absolutely sure, so we spoke to the Whacko Bros…"

Sidney's face drops.

"The Whacko Bros., as you know, are currently under arrest for the suspected murder of Michael Ali. Well, they had a different take on what you two had been discussing…"

"Wait. They weren't anywhere near us. How could they have any idea of what we were talking about?"

"They didn't hear that conversation, but they did tell us that you had discussed the same subject again whilst Younger Whacko was using the facilities at the venue."

…

It was one of those visits where the initial activity had concluded – albeit an unpleasant and unsatisfying activity – but it was very easy to predict that another activity was coming down the pipeline very soon. So, whilst one could conclude one's business and move on to other things, the chances were that the second activity would become imminent almost as soon as he would leave the room that smelled mostly of urine with a slight hint of lemon that was emitted from the urinal cakes. So, it was decision time. Did he get off the toilet and take his chances? Or, did he stay there and await round two? As he was considering this, the door creaks open and in walk two men. It is clear that there are two men involved from the fact that there are two voices conducting a dialogue with each other.

"This is going to be great," a middle-aged, exuberant voice enthuses.

"Yeah. It's, uh…it will be good," a more meek, Indian-sounding voice responded. "This is the opportunity I've been looking for."

Thinking that he will take this opportunity to eavesdrop on the conversation, as he might gain some insight in to the booking of future shows, he makes his decision that he is going to remain seated on the toilet for the long haul.

"Yeah," the older voice continues. "We will get the mayor here – based on the charity angle – and then you will have your opportunity…to do your thing…Kaboom…"

…

"But, that doesn't prove that we were talking about bombing anyone! I was talking about the quality of the show. That's wrestling speak. The show itself will be a huge explosion. Everyone will be talking about it. That's what I meant."

"It may not be clear what you meant," Jake interjects. "But it is clear that you had been speaking to Michael about the mayor being there, when you said that you hadn't spoken about it. This strengthens the witness' statement from earlier, who said they overhead your entire conversation."

Mulligan and Carver can't help but feel smug and satisfied that they have concluded their investigation with such success. However, they try to not show it on their faces. So, instead, there is an awkward silence as they let their words linger in the air. Sidney's face has creased up and he looks down at the table as if it isn't there. Eventually, he looks up at the two police officers, again.

"What does this...mean, then?"

Mulligan takes a deep breath, "It means that we're going to have to keep you in custody until your bond hearing."

Sidney's face changes to a sullen grey disposition.

Mulligan continues, "If I can give you a piece of advice, it would be this. If you confess everything now, in your own words, then it is likely to help you in your trial."

Following one more lengthy pause, Sidney finally gives up and details everything that had led up to the crime and the circumstances of the crime. In fact, he goes into great detail and the process takes well over an hour to complete. At a couple of points during the explanation, Sidney breaks down upon contemplating the state that his life has descended in to. At the end of his description, he breaks down again. He uses the tissues that the police officers have offered him and takes sips of the cooler water that they have prepared for him.

After allowing Sidney to compose himself a bit, but still staring towards the table in front of him, Jake asks, "What I don't understand is, why did you have to go down this road? Why didn't you just leave her?"

"Because, she was all I had. I didn't know what I would do if I lost her," he begins crying again, but manages to eek out, "I still don't."

"I understand that," Jake continues. "That's something that a lot of people face when they're in unhappy or abusive relationships. But it's rare that it ends in attempted murder. Is there something else?"

Sidney's head rises sharply, but then goes back to look at the table.

"Is there another reason why you couldn't break up with her?"

There is another prolonged pause, but Mulligan and Carver know to wait whilst Sidney, with grief in his reddened eyes, works it out in his brain.

"...yeah," Sidney eventually squeaks out, barely audible.

"Yes?" Jake asks. "There is another reason?"

"Yes," Sidney confirms, a little bit louder, this time.

"What is the reason?"

After a couple of false starts where Sidney tries to get the words out, but then stops, he finally responds, "She knows a lot of embarrassing things about me. And she has videos. And photos. Loads of them."

"I know this is hard, Sidney, but: what sort of 'embarrassing things'?"

"Sexual things. Embarrassing things that she made me do. She said she would show them to all my friends in wrestling if I left her."

"Okay. These were on her computer? Her phone?"

"Yeah...all of it."

"Okay. Although you have committed a terrible crime, and there is no way to excuse you for it, it is good that you have let us know this. Well done."

Sidney continues to sit there, shoulders folded in, eyes reddened with tears, looking down towards the edge of the table. Defeated.

...

In the days following the murder of Michael Ali and attempted murder of the South Yorkshire Mayor, Sidney's wife and whomever else was in the Club, that night, the story had exploded on the local, regional and national media. Following the initial reports, each outlet would quickly begin to frame the incident according to their editorial ideology. Much of this focused on professional wrestling being a sleazy, exploitative industry. There were even a number of documentaries under production on the "dark side" of professional wrestling. And a lot of lobbying to local politicians, including the South Yorkshire Mayor, and the national government, including a debate in parliament, on the importance of better regulating professional wrestling in the United Kingdom. Many of the suggestions were so draconian that they would have essentially prevented almost all professional wrestling live events from taking place in the United Kingdom, and only large touring companies, such as WWE, to stage events.

Nonetheless, amidst this storm of rage and indignation, one newspaper article stood out. It was from the national, socialist newspaper The Protector.

PROFESSIONAL WRESTLING REVEALED TO BE 'CESSPIT OF MISOGYNY AND RACISM'

By Thomas Graham

The recent murder of a young man of Bangladeshi origin at a local professional wrestling event in a sleazy South Yorkshire Working Men's Club has brought to light a backwards world of misogyny, racial hatred and bigotry.

One of only two women performing on the show, that night, explained to The Protector how "professional wrestling in this country has had a long sordid history of hatred and mistreatment of women and vilifying other races. If you want to succeed in pro wrestling in the UK as a non-white, you have to become a racial stereotype. If you want to succeed as a woman, you have to be really skinny and dress like a stripper. How is anyone supposed to be taken seriously under those conditions? It has been a cesspit of misogyny and racism."

One look at the posters for the business who promoted these events proves Lizzie Austin's, 23, point with the highlight being that the victim of the crime, Michael Ali, has a rather alarming ring name – "Islamo Kablamo". For many of the posters, there are no women featured on them. When they are featured, their pictures focus on sexual characteristics, such as their breasts or buttocks.

Even though larger companies such as the WWE have recently embraced female wrestling to a greater extent, there is still clearly a long way to go, with many of the female wrestlers being forced to wrestle in skimpy, humiliating outfits and some of the foreign-born wrestlers' nicknames including the likes of 'The Bulgarian Brute' and 'The Sicilian Psychopath'.

When we reached out to WWE for comment, they had the following to say: "Our job here at the WWE is to put smiles on people's faces. We're here to entertain. Our characters are not meant to represent groups of people. They are characters in a show and our audience are aware of that."

Entertainment, it may well be, but it appears that the entertainment that these professional wrestling companies are promoting is stuck in the 1950s.

The Protector reached out to Mr. Sidney, the promoter of the event, for comment, but as he is currently under questioning by police, we were unable to contact him.

…

"Oh, yeah!" bellows a breathy, middle-aged female voice. The tone is indecipherable between the states of distress and jubilation.

The room from which the sound was exclaimed is a well-lit, spacious bedroom in what appears to be a large city flat. The walls from which the scream echoed are painted with neutral colours, the furniture right out of the pages of IKEA. In the far-centre of the room is a bed with a duvet of neutral colours, which is being shuffled back and forth from the activity that is taking place on top of it.

On top of the bed, is a middle-aged woman who appears to be exceptionally fit and healthy for her age, and underneath, a hipster-looking, slim man. As the woman slides back and forth on top of the man, her exclamations continue, shortening in intervals.

"Oh, yeah!"

"Just like that!"

"Ooh! Tom!"

Eventually, the sounds become unintelligible and replaced by monosyllabic exclamations of pleasure. Faster and faster, louder and louder. Until it suddenly stops and all that can be heard in its place is heavy breathing from both participants. The woman falls down to lay beside the man and adjusts the pillow below her head.

"You've got such a nicer cock than my husband."

They both laugh.

"Thank God he's going to be locked up, now."

His breath gradually slowing down, Tom replies, "That was a genius idea you had...Not only to get rid of him, but to frame him, make him want to take the fall for you and to get him locked up for the rest of his life."

"Yeah," she nods. "I won't have to deal with him, ever again. I told him I would visit him in prison whenever I could, but I'm not going to. He's a scumbag. He always cared about wrestling more than he cared about me. He was a child that never grew up. A fat, ugly child. Oh, why did I ever marry him?"

"Well, you're free from him, now. My article is getting a lot of traction. Now, everyone thinks even less of wrestling than they did, before. And, all that had to happen was some Jihadi had to get himself killed, which happens every single day."

The woman shuffles on to her side, facing away from the man, and pours out two glasses of wine from her bedside table. She turns back around and hands one to Tom, keeping the other for herself. She wraps her left arm around Tom like a cushion to prop his head up. Holding her glass up with her right hand, she says, "Here's to our future!"

The couple clink their glasses together and take a sip.

Printed in Great Britain
by Amazon